Maxine the Queen Blogger Plays Chess

Maxine
The Queen Blogger
Plays Chess

A Clever and Mostly True Story
of the Perfect Mate-Check

I0456983

-Naylene-

An Imprint of Black Swan Publications, LLC
Denver, CO

Black Swan Publications, LLC

i.

Maxine the Queen Blogger Plays Chess

Copyrighted Material 2018

The author using the pseudonym "Naylene" has asserted her rights under the U.S. Copyright, Designs and Patents Act to be the identified author of record of this work under the original title "The Choices That We Make".

All rights reserved. No part of this book may be reproduced or transmitted in any form without written permission of the author, except by a reviewer who may quote brief passages for review purposes only.

"Maxine the Queen Blogger Plays Chess
A Clever and Mostly True Story of the Perfect Mate-Check" is a novel read that is mostly true… and somewhat fictional.

Although none of the parties were without fault, their names, blog name and references to locations have been changed to protect their identities anyway.

Cover Art graphic licensed through fotosearch and modified by author.

ISBN (international paperback):13: 978-0-9996515-0-6

Maxine the Queen Blogger Plays Chess

For

"GG"

and

all the Queens who have told an "Amateur"

"Bye"

Maxine the Queen Blogger Plays Chess

Introduction

Dear Reader,
With this first novel, you are being introduced to Maxine and the first of many of her adventures that you can read about in forthcoming novels.

In this first installment of the "Maxine" series, you will get an enteraining glimps into the inner-thoughts of a woman, like many women in some respects, and unlike many women in others.

Betrayal in this case, hurts Maxine like it does most women. However, unlike in many circumstances of a lover's betrayal, Maxine gains the upper-hand, while keeping her cool, her dignity and her heart intact.

Maxine takes her blog readers along on the journey from love lost, to life-found, while keeping her betrayer scrambling unsuccessfully to do damage-control.

Maxine the Queen Blogger Plays Chess

Table of Contents

Maxine
The Queen Blogger
Plays Chess

Maxine the Queen Blogger Plays Chess

"Maxine"

Maxine the Queen Blogger Plays Chess

Maxine had uprooted herself from all her friends and family to join her boyfriend Ben, in a sleepy, isolated East coast town. Ben had accepted an opportunity for a job-transfer, so sight unseen he moved to the town from Denbary, the hip West Coast town they had been living in for years.

Both Maxine and Ben thought a change-of-scenery would be exciting and the move might provide a desperately needed, renewed energy for their relationship.

They had been together a number of years but, this was the first time that they would live together in the small apartment Ben was renting.

Not knowing anyone in the town, made Maxine feel like an outsider. It did not take long for her to feel like the walls of the cramped apartment were closing in on her too.

Maxine tried to convince Ben that they should move to a larger place since the real-estate market was in their favor. Even though they had lived competing for physical and mental space and it was working both their nerves, Ben was content to keep doing so. He was not interested in purchasing a house as an investment. Nor, was he interested in renting something that would give them more space.

Maxine thought it was strange because Ben had been heavily into real estate acquisitions when they lived in Denbary. He had always advised her that "it is better to own your home than to rent it." She knew that money was not the reason for his hesitation.

Ben was quite good at managing his money. He would often say that he was not the type "to throw money away on rent",

Maxine the Queen Blogger Plays Chess

which was a dig at Maxine, who apparently was the type since she'd never owned her own home. Maxine did not like to be anchored down to anything or anyone. Plus, she liked to be able to move about the world without worrying about what might be going on with a house in her absence.

Although he was mostly a home-body, Ben was also a gregarious sort of guy. When not at home, he liked to flaunt his wealth of knowledge of obscure and interesting bits of information at a local pub or bar. He could hold an audience-especially women patrons- captive, while he downed beer like water. No one was ever a stranger to Ben for long.

There were times when Maxine thought Ben was overly gregarious and too open. In fact, Ben talked a lot. Sometimes his constant chatter took too much of Maxine's energy to humor.

Maxine too, had the gift of gab. Unlike Ben though, she was more selective about with whom she shared her gift. Part of what drove her need for a bigger place, was so that she could have a space to retreat to from the noise that Ben created. A room, where she could play her music and entertain her own thoughts.

Since moving, Ben had pretty much become her sole companion-*but, not her soul companion.* She needed more in her world, but she was finding it difficult to meet the kind of people that she had interests in common.

There wasn't much diversity in the new town either. Maxine liked diversity-not just in cultural backgrounds-but also in thought and activity-offerings. The small town was located too far from a major city and that made travel to festivals, concerts and even decent restaurants a hassle to do on a regular basis.

Maxine was attractive, sexy, adventurous, well-read, and well-traveled, as was Ben. Their fondness for travel had attracted them to each other initially. However, Ben was very practical whereas, Maxine was a romantic. She couldn't help but think, that Ben was the one who lacked the passion that made their relationship passion-less.

Their differences were magnified of late, so much so, that Maxine had the pressing concern that they were now complete opposites. Some opposites attract, and some opposites repel. Maxine felt they had come to the latter.

Since moving, Maxine often wondered why she made the move for a relationship that she thought was becoming increasingly tenuous. Maxine had known for a long time that Ben was not "the one" but, he was a good guy, and that counted for a lot in the grand scheme of things.

For the most part, they had as much fun together that they could considering their circumstances. Most importantly, they took care of business. Among other things, Ben had taught Maxine a lot about creating wealth and managing finances. Ben had always stressed the importance of keeping one's eye on his or her money.

Now, in her early 30's, Maxine reflected on how she had spent the better part of her 20's with Ben. She thought a lot about whether she had given him her best years. She wondered whether her best "love" years were still to come.

Maxine the Queen Blogger Plays Chess

She hoped on hope that they were still to come. If truth be told though, she knew that for her, those best years would be shared with a man other than Ben.

In the interim, it was just Ben and Maxine, who would fill each other's days. *Or, so she thought.*

Maxine enjoyed her job and working with most of her co-workers. She and one co-worker in particular, had become friendly, but, their friendship didn't extend outside of their work-place.

It was time Maxine began honestly assessing her life and the longevity of her and Ben's relationship. First though, she needed to secure a place that she could make a home. In doing so, the home would provide her with the space she needed to gain clarity, and to figure out how to redirect her or their course.

So, having secured a decent-paying job, and after three years in the small apartment, Maxine decided that she would become the type to be a home-owner after all. She would purchase a house-*with or without Ben.*

It was also during her time of loneliness, and deep contemplation that Maxine stumbled upon the new concept of Blogging. Blogging seemed the perfect outlet for a lonely girl with a grand imagination and a gift for gab. Maxine quickly got up herself up-to-speed on the ins and outs of how to "Blog".

Being much too private a person to use her real name, Maxine set up her blog under a pseudonym. She thought that if she had anonymity, she could be much more creative and forthcoming about her opinions, musings, and desires.

At the very least, she could share more on her blog than she was able to share with Ben.

It was not that Ben wasn't open-minded. He was open to all kinds of things. It was just that he never really seemed open-minded about the things she was interested in.

Every time Maxine would suggest doing something that was of interest to her, Ben would decline. Yet, he expected her to accompany him when he suggested doing something. There was no longer any give from Ben. He just expected Maxine to take what he offered and for her to be grateful for the offer of his time.

Maxine was a people-watcher. She prided herself on being a quiet observer of the dynamics between people and the spaces they were in. She believed that studying such dynamics, made her highly emotionally intelligent.

Maxine was skilled at bringing the mundane to life through her writing. The blog was a great space to write about her observations about the people she encountered in, around, and about the small town they lived in.

Since a "mundane" life, had become her status quo, the blog was a testament of her ability to make the boring sound interesting and engage an unknown audience.

Maxine thought, "Even if no one reads my posts, or knows they are mine, at least I have an outlet to speak my thoughts aloud." Also, by blogging anonymously, Maxine could express what she really thought about Ben and their relationship.

Blogging also eased some of her frustrations, so she wouldn't take them out on him. Maxine was considerate like that.
Since Maxine hadn't found a good gal-pal to confide in, her blog became a great substitute for one in her time of need. A time, when Maxine had come to realize that the "understanding" she and Ben had, was suddenly open to interpretation.

Maxine felt that when in a relationship, there are certain ground rules players must agree too. While Ben and Maxine did not have many rules to constrain their relationship, they did have three:

1) Each other would always come first 2) They would always be honest with the other if one or both of them wanted to pursue a little something "extra" and 3) If "extra" had the potential to become "in place of", then an honest conversation was immediately in order.

No matter how painful it might be to have that conversation, it could not be avoided.

There were other little "understandings" along the way that they allowed for, but the three rules were cardinal...*at least in Maxine's mind.* There was too much to be lost if they were not agreed upon and written in stone.

Apparently though, Ben was no longer on the same page as Maxine. So, he had added a fourth rule: "There are no rules." Maxine discovered Ben's new rule in a most interesting way—a way that would change Maxine's playbook forever.

Maxine the Queen Blogger Plays Chess

At the time this story takes place, Maxine and Ben had been living for a few months in the fixer-upper she had bought. Her first order of business had been to create what she referred to as her "Tranquility" room, which also acted as her home office.

After she finished setting-up her Tranquility room, Maxine had caught the reno-bug. Fixing up the rest of the split-level, mid-century modern house, became Maxine's priority. Once the house was completed, she told herself, she would broach Ben about their future plans to see if they were mutual.

In between fixing the up the house, Maxine continued writing musings in her blog about the new neighborhood they'd moved to.

Maxine was excited to have a fly new space to spread-out in and call her own. She would soon learn though, that it takes more than owning a grand home, to make it a happy one.

"The Readers"

Maxine the Queen Blogger Plays Chess

Maxine would write about interesting things that she'd observed at work, work-related conferences, about her travels or just going about her day. She would also write short-stories.

Some stories were erotic in nature. Her style of erotica was of the sexy and sensuous type with plot lines, not the nasty kind that was only about the act itself.

To her surprise, without marketing her blog, Maxine had developed a considerable following. Knowing that she had engaged a following, she felt a responsibility to adhere to a decency code though. So, she chose her words very carefully.

As a way to engage her readers, she would begin or end some of the most fantastical blog entries by asking, "Is it True, Mostly True or Completely False?"

The most engaged of her readers would weigh in with their thoughts. She would never confirm what was true or what was her imagination or any combination of the two.

Maxine would write often about her musings on the topic of "Love". Sometimes love truly did "blind" people to realities, because they wanted too badly to believe the lies.

Both men and women became dependent on what lies could sustain, if only they just looked the other way. Too many women though, became emotional and romanticized. They were unwilling to see the forest for the trees. They adopted a sense of security by adapting to lies.

In Maxine's mind, too many women did not set themselves up for that rainy day that would turn into a torrential downpour. They did not think "in case" or "what if?" to prepare themselves for *that* day, the day, that they discovered their sense of security was false.

Maxine could never be accused of that, *at least never again; she could not.* What if being on-guard meant that she might never let her guard down again? What if it meant that she might be exhausted for years from always being on alert? What if it meant that she might never fully trust anyone *ever* again?

Maxine weighed the consequences of "trusting blindly" vs. "being on-guard." In her heart, she knew, or at least hoped-that eventually, she would find a middle ground between the two.

There were no guarantees in relationships. But, it was guaranteed that with "trust" alone, if she did end up in the same place she found herself now, it would be without a house, without money, without options-without a paddle.

How many stories had been written about that?!!! Maxine decided that she would use her blog not only to entertain her readers, but to educate them as well!

She fancied herself having enough worldly, traumatic, and adventurous experiences to have gleaned enough lessons from them to share. She would use her blog to offer some good advice now and then to her readers.

Maxine thought it interesting that complete strangers could be so engrossed in her stories. Her women readers readily empathized with Maxine. They began to eagerly anticipate each entry to read about what Maxine would do next or had already done.

Maxine the Queen Blogger Plays Chess

As a lead-in to stories that she'd written with a particularly salient message in mind, she would invite her readers to get comfortable and have some "Tea".

"The Tea" Day 1, Part 1:
Lunch

Maxine the Queen Blogger Plays Chess

Occasionally, Maxine and Ben had mail trickle into their new address that was forwarded from their old address. One day, Maxine opened a piece of forwarded mail that would prove to be a *third-eye*-opening experience for her.

At the time it had arrived, she had thought it another piece of junk mail disguised as personal correspondence. She noticed that the post-mark was from in-town. Since she didn't know anyone in town that would write her, she didn't rush to open it. Instead, she'd stuck it in her backpack along with that month's "TheStyle" magazine to read later.

While at work a few days later, Maxine went to retrieve her lunch from her backpack and grabbed the magazine to read as well.

Not often, but occasionally, Maxine would eat her lunch in the conference room with her co-workers. She would feign participation in the lunchtime-chatter, but mostly she would sit quietly, read, and eat.

This day would be no different for her. *Or, so she thought.* Maxine proceeded to warm-up the left-overs from the previous night's dinner. The same dinner by-the-way, that Ben had remarked, "Ummm, yum, chicken, again."

Ben frequently made snide remarks about her cooking. He said she never cooked, which she did almost nightly. Or, he said that she only cooked chicken and had a hundred different ways to cook it.

The last bit was partly true. Maxine did have a hundred ways to cook chicken, thanks to her cookbook "A Hundred Ways to Cook Chicken".

Maxine the Queen Blogger Plays Chess

Yet, chicken was not *all* she cooked. Ben's sarcasm about her cooking was meant as a little jab. They had been hammering each other with little jabs a lot lately.

She sat down to wait for her lunch and opened her magazine to page one. She began reading through it. She loved TheStyle magazine, and pored over each month's copy, page-by-page, ad-by-ad.

Maxine was a bit of a thrift-store fashionista. She was always looking for recommendations from the magazine as to what was "in-the-now". With the tips she gleaned from the pages, she'd look for similar pieces but, from different eras and in her favorite thrift-stores.

Then, by adding those pieces to her collection of timeless pieces, she created a uniquely stylish wardrobe with a twist of vintage. Maxine's wardrobe was thus, always fresh and on-point.

Wedged between pages 21 and 22 is where she found the mail that she had stuck in her backpack days before. To get it out of the way, she opened the mail, fully prepared for it to be junk-mail that she could throw away.

She was not prepared, *to say the least*, for what the contents of a genuine, hand-written letter spelled-out.

"The Tea" Day 1, Part 2:
The Letter

Maxine the Queen Blogger Plays Chess

"Dear Maxine," the letter began.

"You may not remember me, but we met at Brooklyn and Steve's party a few months ago. I have some information that I've been holding onto, because I couldn't decide what, or if I should do anything with it.

I finally decided that even if you get mad, I should tell you, because I just couldn't let a sistah go out like this. Then, I couldn't decide whether I should write you or find your number to call you. Ultimately, I thought this letter was best.

"What the hell?!" Maxine thought, as she continued reading.

I know that what I am about to tell you will hurt you. I'm sorry, but knowledge is power. I hope you will use this knowledge powerfully.

A month ago, I saw Ben in a very compromising position. He was driving, leaving Littonton. A woman was giving him head as he drove.

I know it was him because I know his car. I also recognized the profile of his chiseled jawline immediately. To be honest, I have wanted to get with him myself. So, I know his striking good-looks. (You know there are not that many good-looking men around here, so they stand-out.)

Anyway, at first Ben looked like he was talking to himself. I was trying to speed up to catch his big, brown eyes- you know- just to say hello is all. That's when I noticed what looked like the top of a woman's head in his lap.

Surprised, I hung back so that he wouldn't see me-but I followed him.

Maxine the Queen Blogger Plays Chess

After a few minutes, her head popped up, so I switched to the passenger-side to have a look at her. That is when I recognized her. Her name is Dawn, and she works in the accounting department for J. P. Clark and Bagger.

Maxine, I never would have figured Ben to cheat on you because of all that you have going for yourself. Not only that, Dawn is not even cute! Girl, I could not believe my eyes!

You are truly a beautiful woman and the envy of many women in town. You must believe that, even if doubt sets in. Also, know that men are men. Work that knowledge to your advantage.

Again, I am so sorry to tell you this about Ben. You can do what you want with the information, but I just thought that you should know. There are just too many men out here playing us dirty!

*I didn't want you to be blind-sided and have to go through some "Exhale" type drama. You can do some research, but believe me when I say, I know her, and **you** have the upper hand on so many levels.*

It all comes down to the choices that we make. You are in a position to choose. Choose wisely.

Sincerely,
Anonymous

Maxine sat mesmerized and breathless by "The Letter". She was unsure of whether to be thankful to "Anonymous" or pissed at her. Who was she?

She scrutinized "Anonymous's" hand-writing. Maxine didn't recognize it. She noticed though, that it was curvaceous and jaunty in script. Maxine had taken a handwriting analysis class out of personal interest once. She could tell by the script that "Anonymous" was confident and orderly without being uptight.

Was "Anonymous" saying this to cause trouble between Maxine and her man, so that they would break up? Then, she could swoop in on Ben? Was "Anonymous" genuinely "looking out for a sistah"? Was "Anonymous" trying to get even with Dawn? "Who does this sort of thing!?" Maxine wondered.

The microwave beeped and brought Maxine back to the moment. Whoever she was, "Anonymous" did not sound like anyone Maxine knew. She thought back to a few months ago. Maxine recalled meeting people at a couple of parties that Ben had received invites to.

There was no one that she remembered connecting with though. Well, there was that one woman…Maxine thought back to a woman she'd met. The woman was the wife of one of Ben's colleagues. "What the hell?!" She thought again.

Maxine regained her breath and quickly shoved the letter back into the envelope, and then back in-between the pages of her magazine. She looked around to see if any co-workers had noticed her reaction. It appeared that they had not.

Maxine felt like her lunch-hour was over, but in reality, it had only been 15 minutes. She was no longer hungry. She packed-up her stuff and went back to her office. Once inside, she did what she rarely did. She closed the door and sat at her desk with her head in her hands.

A strange sensation was coursing through her body. She was not going to cry, as one might expect getting that kind of news. No, she was steely. Her nerves were hardened rather than on edge. The news embarrassed her. Not so much because Ben was with another woman, but because he did not respect her enough to be more discreet about it.

Now, an outsider was privy to his cheating and to her embarrassment. Maxine was seething mad at that. She took a couple of deep and slow breaths to get her racing-heart back to a normal pace.

She thought, and she thought. She finally concluded that she and Ben had trust and honesty as the cornerstone of their relationship. She would give him the benefit of doubt that was warranted after nine years together.

She would simply just ask him about it. She decided that she would wait until she got home to ask him though. She did not want her co-workers to hear, if things got ugly.

"The Tea" Day 1, Part 3:
The Waiting Game

Maxine the Queen Blogger Plays Chess

At any given time, Maxine was very controlled and put together. In many respects, she was a SCU-a Self-Contained-Unit. She rarely asked anyone for help and kept herself self-sufficient that way. Of course, even being controlled, it was not easy for her to sit on the information she'd received that day. Thus, she had to dig into her emotional reserves to stay together.

Many times, during that afternoon, she had reached to pick-up the phone to call Ben.

On her last attempt, when she began to dial, something inside her told her, "Wait. Calm down. Think this through a little bit more." Deeply connected to her ancestors, she often sought called on them for guidance. Maxine felt that they were the "something inside her" that was speaking to her. She heeded their words.

Maxine let the phone rest. She continued with her work of designing media-campaigns for a local non-profit. She tried to focus on the gratification she received by knowing that the campaigns she designed, would bring-in much-needed funding to her organization.

The funding would support community programs that focused on children and women at-risk of domestic violence and other forms of abuse. However, even that gratification, was not enough to distract her from "The Letter".

Maxine again tried hard to think of who "Anonymous" could be. She didn't have any friends in town close-enough to protect her interests like a "sistah" would.

Maxine the Queen Blogger Plays Chess

In fact, Maxine often lamented to Ben, that even though she had moved there over three years-ago, she hadn't found any women her age to connect with. Sure, in passing, she'd met a couple of women who were smart and on the ball.

However, as soon as they realized how boring and remote the town was, they jetted. It usually only took about 1 month to figure it out. Once they did, Maxine was left to her own devices once again. Her devices namely being, a computer and a Blog.

Maxine thought about how she could sure use a friend at the moment. She wondered if she was over-looking a friend in "Anonymous". Try as she might though, she just couldn't think of anyone who knew her and Ben well-enough, to know that they had it going on.

Ben had more of a social scene through his job. The parties they went to were often lively, but Maxine believed the people a bit strange. She had once remarked to Ben, that she thought a lot of his co-workers were Swingers.

The men wanted to know too much about her and were too flirty. The women seemed to size her up, at the same time, they were cozying up to Ben. He laughed it off when she talked about his co-workers. "You're new blood. You're pretty and you're closed. Of course, that will pique their interests." He would say.

She would press him with, "Well, what about the flirting they do with you right in front of my eyes? It is disrespectful. I'm sure you've told them plenty of my business, but you must not have told them, I don't play that shit."

Maxine the Queen Blogger Plays Chess

"Max, relax. We all work together in high-stress jobs. We have a familiarity with each other from the workplace. Naturally, that extends to after work sometimes. That's when we can let down our guard with each other. It's nothing and they mean you no offense."

"Hmmm." was all that Maxine replied. In her heart-of-hearts, she didn't really care. She did not press Ben more, because she didn't want him to think it was about him. With Ben's ego, he was prone to take her questioning as a sign of jealously and that would stroke his already huge ego.

Maxine wasn't jealous. For Maxine, it was about respect. It was being disrespected that raised her ire. Ben was either to affable or spineless, to keep his co-workers in check. This meant she had to do it.

On a couple of occasions, she was about to give one of his co-workers an earful of warning. Before she could though, Ben would read the look on her face and pre-empt her with some of his gregarious charm. He had come to know that he would much rather put them in check, than have Maxine do it. His passivity really irked her. She was digressing though.

Maxine thought long and hard. Ultimately, she couldn't see anyone she'd met at one of Ben's work gatherings, as looking out for her. She could however, very well see "Dawn" as one of his flirtatious colleagues.

"No. Anonymous had said this Dawn-chick worked at a different company all-together from Ben." Maxine shook her head and said aloud. This made Maxine wonder how Ben and Dawn had met—*and when.*

Maxine the Queen Blogger Plays Chess

She looked at the clock and was glad to see it was quitting time. Maxine wanted to get home to her tranquility room. She would have the house to herself for about two-hours before Ben came home. Maybe once she arrived there, she could have a good cry. Maybe, that cry would bring her some clarity.

When Maxine got home, she went to her tranquility room and laid down on her sofa. She stared up at the ceiling for a long time, waiting for the tears to fall. She wanted to cry, but the tears wouldn't come.

So, she turned over and took a cat-nap. She awoke more refreshed. She immediately outlined her next steps.

Maxine prided herself on being able to keep a secret. In fact, many people had confided all sorts of things to her without her asking. She was known to honor requests for confidentiality.

Even strangers seemed to be drawn to her and poured out their business. She thought to herself, "If I can be tight-lipped about other people's business, then even though it will be an excruciating wait, I can be tight-lipped about mine!"

Now that her eyes were wide-open, instead of confronting Ben with "The Letter" when he got home, Maxine decided she would remain tight-lipped about it. She felt the ancestors would let her know when the time was right.

Maxine decided she would watch Ben more closely over the next couple of days. Or, however long she could stand not asking him about Dawn. She would consider herself a spy in her own home and do some intel-gathering in the interim.

Maxine the Queen Blogger Plays Chess

To help keep her mind focused on something other than Ben's sordid affair, Maxine spent some time writing a few engaging observations for her blog,

When Ben came home that evening, (later than usual she noticed) she had already eaten dinner. "What smells good?" He asked. She indicated that she had left him some *Beef Stroganoff* warming in the oven.

"Thanks!" He said. He went into the kitchen, made a plate, grabbed a few beers, and proceeded upstairs. Aren't you going to watch TV with me?" She asked. "I can't. I have to check my email to see if a bid came through from a potential contractor. After I square things away and shower, I'll come down."

Ben bounded up the stairs leaving Maxine looking suspiciously after him from the couch. "Hmmm, he just left work, but needs to check his email?" Maxine silently thought to herself. After an hour of TV watching, Ben hadn't reappeared. Maxine cleaned up the kitchen, then called her mom to see how she was doing.

They talked for forty-minutes or so. Maxine decided not to tell her mom about "The Letter". Her mom would begin to worry and take on stress needlessly. Maxine would fill her in, when she had the situation under control.

After she got off the phone, Maxine realized that it had been almost 2 hours and Ben had never come back down-not even for another beer.

Maxine went upstairs and saw that their bedroom door was closed. She opened it and found Ben asleep on their bed with his cell-phone lying next to him. His dinner dishes with barely touched food, were on the night-table.

Although Ben was in a deep slumber and wouldn't hear her, she quietly took the dishes downstairs, washed them, and returned to their room. She quietly climbed into bed and tried to go to sleep as well, but couldn't.

One reason was because, Ben was snoring loudly. *As he was prone to do.* His snore wasn't just loud though, it was obnoxious. It was so unrhythmic that although she tried to sleep next to him, she just couldn't find a wave-length that she could sync with that would lessen the obnoxiousness.

Then, too, she also knew that she would toss and turn with her mind going over the day's events. Also, it was not yet 10pm. If she went to sleep this early, she would wake-up earlier than necessary and just toss and turn until it was time to get ready for work.

Maxine did what she usually did when she couldn't sleep. She got up and went to her tranquility room. She'd furnished it with a sofa-bed for precisely such occasions. She didn't lay down though. She turned on her computer and reached up for the vase that was sitting high on a book shelf.

It had been so long since Ben had brought home flowers for her, that she felt the vase was a safe place to keep her external hard-drive. She reached in, pulled it out and plugged it into her computer.

She opened her secret file of blog-posts that she'd previously written. She liked to have some on-the-ready, for when she had writer's block, or there was just nothing to speak of that she could make into an exciting blog post.

She opened a blog-entry titled "Cohabitation Sucks!" She had written the post when she and Ben were first moved-in together in his small apartment.

Maxine had, had a difficult period of adjustment. Everything Ben did, worked her every nerve. It was his snoring that she had written about at the time. She thought it fitting for the post to see the light now. She updated a few details, then copied and pasted it into her blog. Then, she checked to see if there had been any comments about her last post.

In her last blog-entry, she had written about a work-conference she'd been to that was held in another county over. She remarked how different the scenery was in that county. There was one gentleman in attendance, that had particularly caught her eye.

He was a big, handsome man. His size was quite sexy to Maxine. He was tall and muscular, but not overly so. He had some fluff to him as well. She had titled the blog-entry "Mountaineering Man".

"Mountaineering Man" was also the name of a chocolate-candy delivery service in her area. Mountaineering Man would come to the offices with a cart loaded with various chocolate candies for sale. It was a rare day that Maxine could resist the temptation to purchase her favorite chocolate-covered toffee balls.

In her post, she had compared the two "chocolates" and wondered if the "Mountaineering Man" she'd spied at the conference would deliver some of his chocolate to her on-the-regular too.

A few readers had commented that she should be careful about getting a "sugar-rush" at his altitude, and that maybe she needed "to check for diabetes" since she was such a chocoholic.

Maxine had a few chuckles, responded to them in her witty fashion and logged-out of her blog. She quickly checked her emails, then shut-down her computer for the night and placed the hard-drive back in the vase. She laid down on her sofa and went to sleep.

"The Tea" Day 2, Part 4:
"Can't Hardly Wait"

Maxine the Queen Blogger Plays Chess

The next morning, as Maxine was picking out her outfit for the day, Ben sat up in bed and pensively watched her. "Good morning." Maxine greeted him. "Good morning." He replied. "Listen," he started nervously. "I'm going to go with some co-workers to watch the game at the pub after work."

The "Pub" was a local watering-hole that was popular with the locals. When there was a game of any sort, basketball, baseball, football, professional or college-sometimes, even a local high-school game, it seemed the whole town could be found there watching it.

The town was too small to have any professional teams of its own to root for, so they whole-heartedly supported teams from others states and universities. Maxine said, "Oh? What time are you going? I'll meet you there."

Ben's eyes widened, and she thought she saw a flash of panic in them. "What?" He said incredulously but tried to act nonchalantly. "You don't even like sports, or bars for that matter."

"I know." Maxine said, as she pulled on a skirt. "I just thought it would be nice to do something together. It's been a while since we've been out." "With each other." She quickly clarified. "It'll be fun."

Ben hesitated. "No. I don't think so." Maxine kept getting dressed. "Yes, it will. What time are you getting there?" Ben responded sharply with "I won't go then." Maxine looked at him surprised, and said, "Jeez. Ok. Fine. Go ahead. I won't go." Then, she grabbed her shoes and went downstairs to pack her lunch.

Maxine the Queen Blogger Plays Chess

"If that place wasn't so small, I'd show up anyway!" She fumed silently. It *was* small though, and she didn't want Ben to throw a hissy-fit when he saw her there. Plus, she could not spy very well, if she was in plain sight.

Maxine was even more determined now to find out "What the hell, is Ben up to?" She gathered her things and headed out to work, without telling Ben goodbye.

At work, she went through the motions of doing her job, but she couldn't get their last exchange out of her mind. She decided that she'd waited long enough. She had enough "evidence" to confirm that Ben was indeed up to something.

She was going to find out what and right now. She closed the door to her office. She sat at her desk and took a few deep breaths.

"The Tea" Day 2, Part 5:
"The Phone Call"

Maxine the Queen Blogger Plays Chess

"Guide me ancestors!" Maxine prayed silently to herself. Then she reassured herself, "Things won't get ugly." as she called Ben on his cell phone. Ben answered her call on the second ring and with a smart remark. "Hello, All-Knowing One!" Maxine paused silently, "Wow!   Finally, some appropriate sarcasm." She thought. "It's funny you should call me that." She said.

"What's up?" He asked. "Not much." She said, as her heart pounded. "What are you doing?" She asked. "Oh, I'm just about to go inside this drugstore and pick up a few toiletries." Ben spoke as if their tense conversation this morning had not happened. Ben was passive like that. He never let things weigh on his mind for long-*if at all.*

Considering the time, it seemed Ben should have been at work. "Aren't you working today?" Maxine asked. "Yeah, I just had a few extra minutes on my hands, so I am running some errands." He said lightly.

Maxine straightened up and said, "Listen, I want to ask you something." She got straight to the point. "Are you seeing anyone?"

"What!? No! Where is that coming from?" Ben asked, with the shock in his voice telling all. "Hmmm." Maxine murmured. "I have some information that says you are. I just want to know if it's true?" She said casually. "Absolutely not!" He exclaimed.

Maxine coolly explained, "Ben, remember. We said we would be honest with each other, so you don't have to lie. I have some information that says you are seeing someone. I just want an honest answer. Is it true?"

Maxine the Queen Blogger Plays Chess

"What information? Who told you that? When was I supposedly with someone else? Where did someone say I was?" Ben rattled off several questions without taking a breath.

She could tell by the winded register of his voice, that he was at once trying to deny, and figure out how she knew--the truth.

Maxine's heart sank for a moment. Then she said, "Ok, Ben, we'll talk about this later." "No, let's talk about this now!" He demanded. "Nooo." She said drawing out the word for emphasis. "I am at work. I am not going to talk about this, so everyone can hear. We will talk about it later."

"Ok, I'll talk to you about this when I get home." Ben conceded reluctantly.

"That Bastard!" Maxine said to herself as she hung up the phone. "That Witch!" She said aloud. Maxine was hot! She also was not sure who was the bigger witch, "Anonymous" or "Dawn".

"The Tea" Day 2, Part 6:
"Maxine's Money"

Maxine the Queen Blogger Plays Chess

Maxine took a break to take a quick walk. She hoped the chilly weather would help her cool-off. She went to her bank, which fortunately, was just a couple of blocks away from her office. The town was so small, it seemed pretty-much everything, was "just a couple of blocks away".

Maxine walked and thought and thought and walked. "Who was this Dawn?" she wondered. She thought back to her and Ben's conversations over the last few months, and this morning.

If she was honest with herself, Maxine had suspected something was up with Ben for a while. She just wasn't sure, given their location.

After all, there was no one hot in their town- *except for them.* Yes, he had been known to lower his standards before. Maxine reminded herself of a couple of those times. When they lived in Denbary, there were better choices that were easily had-- but he didn't make them.

"But, around here, he would have to lower them so low, as to settle with someone akin to a gutter rat. A toothless one at that!" She exclaimed aloud.

"Would Ben stoop that low *again*? Was he that desperate?" She asked herself, disbelieving he would or that he was. Then she thought again. Ben didn't look for someone who would require work. He homed in on the dumb and easy type- *Maxine, being the exception. Of course.*

Ben was also the type that would look even if things were perfect. He needed the ego stroke of knowing he could get a woman-even if she weren't hard for anyone to get. Ben would seek out the type of woman that was so desperate for affection that she would do anything to get it. Especially, if she could stroke her own ego by managing to get "it" from a good-looking guy like Ben.

Considering his middle-age, most anyone of interest to him would be younger. Ben always said, "I would never date a woman my age or older."

Maxine was several years younger. Then again, now that she knew that Ben was a liar, she would not rule out an older woman. The town they had moved to, seemed to offer either a really young or a really old crowd. Finding someone in the middle was difficult-*she knew from personal experience.*

The next town over, Littonton, offered a little bit more of a selection. Housing was more expensive but the location was closer for those who commuted to the big-city for work.

"Given the information in the letter, this chick was probably not another town over, if Ben had been seen leaving it with Dawn." Maxine rationalized.

A few times, Ben had jokingly said things like, "I need a girlfriend. Can I have a girlfriend?" Or, "I had a great day today!" An exclamation which was completely contrary to his usual moaning and groaning about work.

When Ben had a "great day", Maxine understood it as code that someone had flirted with him. A great day meant that his ego had been given a nice stroke. She didn't mind. Her ego was stroked often.

Maxine the Queen Blogger Plays Chess

Ego-strokes did feel good-even if they led to nothing more than a fleeting feeling. They felt good even if they were from someone Maxine would not even dream of getting with.

One day, Ben said that he'd met an attractive woman at one of his sales locations. He said that she had pretty Black skin. "Her skin looked so smooth and buttery", that he wanted to reach out and touch it.

Maxine could appreciate how pretty she must be and gave her the code-name "Velveteen". Ben said, "That name is fitting." Maxine didn't feel threatened by "Velveteen's" beauty. Afterall, Maxine's own youthfully-smooth and melanated skin-tone was on and poppin too.

Occasionally, she would conspiratorially play along with Ben. She'd ask, "Did you see Velveteen today?" He would just smile. Eventually, Ben would tell Maxine that her actual name was Isis. Isis, as it turned out, was into women and was not thinking about Ben. "So, umm, then, you must have asked her out?" Maxine half stated, and half questioned.

"No." Ben said. "One day when I went to make a sales-call, I saw her kissing her girlfriend or some woman in the parking lot. She saw me, waved and went right back to it."

Ben thought he was a magnate for any and everyone. Maxine could tell that Ben was a bit deflated by the news. "He's seriously disappointed, his charm didn't pique Isis' curiosity *at-all*. Cocky S.O.B." Maxine smiled at the thought of his ego being taken down a notch.

Whenever Ben would bring up anything that remotely seemed like he was sniffing around for something new, something strange, or verging on a confession that he'd found it, Maxine would listen-in closely. She would ask him questions and appear to be as open to the possibilities as he was.

At the time, Maxine noted Ben's information about Isis, as a sign that he was indeed sniffing around for something. Or, maybe, he'd already found it. Maybe, Maxine thought, he was really just trying to throw her off his trail with that story. "Hmmm." Maxine pondered that for a minute.

Then too, for someone who had no interest in computers, he had been checking his email *a lot* lately. She knew this because he used her computer to do it. She thought it was for his work. Maxine often had to shoo Ben out of her Tranquility room, so she could get to her blog.

Long after any mention of Isis had faded to black, Maxine jokingly asked if one of the flirtatious encounters that had him so excited, also had a husband for her! Ben didn't answer.

Maxine had given Ben so many opportunities to seek and ask for what he wanted-*as long as it was within reason*. Maxine did not say anything to him about the ego-strokes she received, because she had her Blog for that.

Maxine sighed and thought, *"If only we stroked each other's egos."* Ben and Maxine were bored. They just needed a small infusion of something unfamiliar, something new, a little somethin-somethin. They had been together a long time. Maybe, they had been together too long.

Maxine the Queen Blogger Plays Chess

Maxine knew first-hand that sometimes, someone else could make things better for them both. She understood. "Damn it!" She said aloud. What she couldn't understand, was why he would lie to her.

She knew that right then, neither was working for each other sexually. Still, she thought that for the most part, their lives with each other were tolerable, if not even good most of the time. Apparently, she was wrong.

"Why did Dawn get the benefit of Ben protecting *her* identity from me?" Maxine fumed. Based on what Maxine knew about Ben's gift-of-gab, and his lack of regard for keeping Maxine's business- *Maxine's* business, she figured that Dawn probably knew loads about her.

It was then that Maxine had an "Ah ha!" moment. Dawn must have someone who she was lying to, as well. It very well may be that Dawn had a husband. "Beautiful…" She thought as she finished her banking and walked back to her office.

"The Tea" Day 2, Part 7:
"The Emails"

Maxine the Queen Blogger Plays Chess

Maxine arrived home to an empty house. She thought that maybe, just maybe given their earlier phone chat, Ben wouldn't go to the bar to watch the game after all and might just bring his ass home early from work.

In the interim, Maxine tried to prepare herself to remain mentally calm because, she knew whenever Ben did arrive, they were going to get to the heart of the matter. To calm and distract her mind, she turned on her computer to check her email and if she had any blog comments.

Many of her followers communicated with her through email, instead of waiting for her to moderate their comments on her blog. She wondered how they felt about her "Cohabitation Sucks!" rant. Her blog was mostly humorous musings and erotic stories, so she rarely got rude comments.

Still, every time she logged on, it was with nervous anticipation of whether the comments would be good, bad, or even racy. Sometimes, she would get a reader who would be so inspired by one of her erotic stories, that he or she, would write her with a racy musing his or her own.

With the kind of days, she'd been having, Maxine really did not want to open more unwelcomed news in the form of a negative critique of a post. Nor, did she want a weird confessional inspired by one. When she went to log-in to her email, she discovered that the account was already logged-in. "That's strange," she thought.

Usually, even if you do not sign out of your Yohey email account, after a certain amount of time, Yohey will log you out automatically. She hadn't been on since last night. She was certain she'd logged out of it then.

Maxine the Queen Blogger Plays Chess

Since she started her blog, Maxine was ever more cautious about logging-out of all her accounts. Still, even if she somehow forgot, it should have logged her off by now. She looked at the account and realized that it was not her account at all.

It was Ben's email account that was logged-in. "Huh?" She thought, momentarily confused. She guessed that Ben must have really been at home when she had called him earlier. Or, maybe he had raced home after she had called him. Perhaps, he intended to destroy any evidence of his cheating-including any emails. Emails, she didn't even have access to-*until now.*

Maxine envisioned Ben hurriedly leaving the house, just before she got home. It had only been an hour or so since they spoke. In his haste, maybe he'd forgotten to log-out. Yohey, must not have logged him out yet.

"What good fortune!" Maxine thought. *If one could call it that.* "This just keeps getting better...*for me.*" She smirked.

Under any other circumstance, out of respect for his privacy, she would have just logged him out without reading his emails. However, mutual respect was no longer something they shared. Therefore, respect for his privacy was no longer a consideration of Maxine's.

She began to read through his emails. At first, she didn't see anything disturbing and felt somewhat relieved. Then, she checked his email "trash" and there they were, as obvious as a red lipstick imprint on a white collar. Evidence. *And, something more. Insurance.*

Maxine the Queen Blogger Plays Chess

Maxine had taught Ben everything *he knew* about computers, including introducing him to email. She did not teach him everything *she knew* about them though (which was considerable). Being relatively new to tech, and really quite unschooled about email, Ben did not know that just because you move an email to the trash, does not mean the trash has been taken out of the house. *So-to-speak.*

Maxine read through the emails. Some emails were pretty innocuous. Others were not so. She confirmed that there was indeed someone named "Dawn" in the picture. The earliest date she could find on an email was four months ago.

It seemed Ben and Dawn had met right around when she was closing on her house. The timing was in-line with Anonymous' dates. Apparently, Ben and Dawn were planning to run off together and into the sunset in the next few months.

At least *Dawn* was planning to. Maxine thought about her money. Ben and Dawn were indeed planning some "Exhale" type drama. Many women had learned a lot from Exhale, including Maxine. *Her stuff was not going down like that!*

Not only were the two planning an exit, but they had also recently spent some time in Littonton, which further gave credence to Anonymous' letter. Maxine also noted that Dawn's email address was from her workplace. It was the same place that "Anonymous" had said she worked.

There was indeed some sexing going on too because Dawn raved about it. "I haven't felt so good in such a long time. You have me fantasizing things I would never have before…things that you make into reality." Dawn gushed in her emails.

Maxine's face was flush as she read more. "Bring a porno film, let's reenact it." "I love your touch." "You are so sweet." "You make me explode." "I can't wait until our trip to San Fran."

"Just think of when the spring comes, and we have each other all the time." "No more worrying about prying eyes." "The way you do that special thing you do to me makes me so…" Maxine paused reading the emails and took a deep breath.

"San Francisco?!" "Spring?!" "That witch!" This was not the "understanding" she and Ben had agreed to. This was *not* "within reason". Maxine was hottttttttttt!

She then checked Ben's "Sent" mail, to see what his side of the story was. Even in the face of indisputable evidence, she was still trying to be fair. Still trying to find him some redemption. But, it was not to be, because when it rains, it pours.

While Dawn would write paragraphs and was particularly telling in them, Ben would respond in typical guy-fashion, with only one or two sentences. However short his responses though, they said a lot. "What a great time I had with you last night." "I can't wait to see you again." "You are so sexy!"

The betrayal hurt, but Maxine forced herself to keep reading what Ben wrote. "It's crappy outside, let's just stay in bed all day and order delivery when we get to the hotel." "I can't wait to see you tonight." "Since I met you, you have, and I have, and we have…" and on the emails went.

"That eff'ing, rat-ass-bastard!" Maxine fumed. She was on fire! She felt like she was having an out-of-body experience. Yet, not so out-of-body that she had taken leave of her stellar-sense.

Maxine thought back to the last time she and Ben had sex-with each other. She was glad it was so long ago she couldn't remember. "Praise the ancestors!" She exclaimed.

Maxine forwarded copies of the emails to a safe place, all the while thinking, "Companies often frown upon employees using company email for personal business. *Especially*, if that personal business is to interfere in someone else's household."

This was personal. Dawn was interfering in Maxine's household. Maxine would bring the witch down. With her, would go Ben. Maxine's mind was racing anew.

She did a little more intel-gathering on the World Wide Web. Then, she began to organize her thoughts once again based on newly acquired information.

"The Tea" Day 2, Part 8:
"Confessions"

Maxine the Queen Blogger Plays Chess

As much as she knew, Maxine still had her unknowns. How deep had this shit gotten between those two? Maxine was particularly mad at herself, for not sensing something sooner.

Or, more accurately, she was incensed with herself, for not acting when she had indeed, sensed something was amiss at home.

She consoled herself with the thought, "In the grand scheme of things, it was not how one fell down that mattered. In the grand-scheme, it was how one gets up that counts in the end."

She had the power to choose what she wanted out of her relationship with Ben. She could choose if she wanted a relationship with him at all. *He may not have a choice.* This thought calmed her.

By the time Ben walked in that evening, Maxine had quite a bit sorted out. What Ben would say to her, would tip the scales to the side of her wrath, or her forgiveness.

Their conversation would determine if she could forgive him. If so, she could scrap the posts she'd been busy writing as 'blog therapy' while she'd waited for him to come home-- which he did not do early.

Or, Ben would determine if the posts would be posted as scheduled and as written. She was being generous in letting Ben decide-*albeit unknowingly* how her next blog entry would be written.

Maxine was calmly sitting at her desk in her Tranquility room, reading a magazine when Ben came in. He asked the usual

Maxine the Queen Blogger Plays Chess

perfunctory questions about how her day was-*as if he didn't know.*

She didn't look-up and continued to feign reading. She answered him, in short replies, eager to get them over with. Maxine wanted to move on to the important business at-hand.

Ben sat down on the couch, grabbed the TV remote, and began to flip casually through the channels, as if nothing was wrong. They were both quiet as she read her magazine and he searched the channels.

After ten minutes, Ben broke the silence by saying, "Well, I guess I'll head to bed now." "Huh! Whoa! Whaaa, What?!" Maxine silently thought, but calmly asked, "Are we going to talk about who you've been seeing?"

Ben replied, "No, because I'm not seeing anyone. I don't know what you heard, but I'm not seeing anyone. There's nothing to talk about. I know you just want an argument, but there is nothing to argue about."

Maxine sat and looked at Ben for a long minute, appraising him without saying anything. She so badly wanted to ask him, "Do you know who you're talking to? Remember me? The woman you have been with for the last nine years. The woman who has withered many, many storms with you?"

Maxine wanted to say, "Look you sorry-ass, spineless MF, we both know the party ain't jump'in like it used to, but just be a man about it." She wanted to scream *"Hello!* It's me, Maxine! I'm not the dumb-ass chick you've been hanging out with of late!"

Maxine the Queen Blogger Plays Chess

Instead, she inhaled softly and lobbied the first of three balls of ammunition. "You know, *Dawn* is not very classy. What kind of woman goes into details about her period-cramps?" Maxine then sarcastically air-quoted one of Dawn's emails, "Not this week, I've got cramps. Out of commission. But you can have it next week."

Before Ben could answer, Maxine did. "A tacky, sloppy, nasty witch, that's who. A nasty skank is more like it." Before Ben could recover from the first lobby-*hearing Dawn's name*, Maxine lobbied her second ball of ammunition-*quotes from their emails*.

Maxine had given Ben enough information to know that she was not in the mood for his games. Out of the kindness of her heart, she had given him a few seconds to think about his response. Now, would Ben continue to lie and deny anything was going on?

Just like a man, yes, he would. Instead of hearing Usher's "Confessions", Maxine suddenly heard Shaggy's "It Wasn't me" playing in her head.

Ben tried to recover. Maxine watched as he failed miserably. Ben glared at her. "You are a piece of work." He spat at her venomously. "Thank you." Maxine said, and smiled (she thought so too).

Then, Ben decided to try a different approach. "I know you hacked into my email!" He accused her. "Emails?" she questioned. "What emails? Emails from whom? How would I know about emails if, (she air quoted him now) '*there's nothing going on*' for them to exist?"

Maxine the Queen Blogger Plays Chess

"You know what? I'm glad that you saw the emails, because you can see, *anyone* can see, that all it was...was a little harmless flirting. There's nothing in them that would suggest otherwise!"

Ben said it like a drowning man who was trying not to acknowledge the water creeping up to his nose, would say it.

"Really? Would that "anyone" include her husband? Maxine casually let ball #3 fly. A look of terror flashed in Ben's eyes. She had made a calculated guess about the husband. Ben's eyes had just confirmed him, for her.

Maxine decided that she'd made enough moves, *for now.* She would not play all of the many cards she held in one night.

It was late. Maxine was exhausted. However, she had just enough energy to end Ben's night with something for him to sleep on. "This isn't the end of the conversation. My house-of-cards fell tonight, but my house-of-cards won't be the only one to fall."

As Ben left her room, she turned to her computer and uploaded blog entries, "*The "Tea"* parts #1-5, as scheduled and as written.

"The Tea" Day 3, Part 9:
"The List"

Maxine the Queen Blogger Plays Chess

"So, Ben wants to play it like that? He wants to *play me*, like that?" Maxine thought at work the next day. "Even though I'm one of the cleverest people Ben knows, he really does want to play me like I'm an idiot." Maxine slowly shook her head.

Over her years, Maxine had come to realize that many people thought that the "quiet ones" were quiet because they did not have a thought in their head to speak of.

People who thought like that, operated in a loud, loquacious manner, and considered themselves to be, and were considered by others to be, bright. Even when they said and did dumb stuff.

Maxine was used to people underestimating her because she wasn't loud or braggadocious. She let them assume what *she* wanted. If she felt compelled to, she would dispel any notions that her intellect was inferior-*at her choosing*.

"So, let him play-dumb and play with me." She thought. "I'll use it to my advantage." She smiled deviously. Maxine was of the school-of-thought that it is "Better to be thought a fool, then to open your mouth and prove it." Obviously, Ben didn't agree because when he opened his mouth, a fool had fallen out.

"Ben is going to play me like that on top of the other playing he is doing." Maxine thought again. "Ok." Maxine took her lunch out of the refrigerator and continued her thought. "I'll play along. This might actually be fun."

Although, it was hardly warm outside, Maxine took her lunch to a nearby park because she needed to think without interruptions. Because of the chilly weather, she easily found a quiet spot to contemplate the situation.

The weather and her situation brought to mind the title "The Coldest Winter Ever". It was one of her favorite books by author and activist, Sista Souljah. The book had nothing to do with what Maxine was going through at the moment. Yet, she laughed aloud because it was Winter, and Maxine was currently in the mind-set to be the coldest she'd ever been.

She took out her headset and mp3 player from her IrreSistahable™ tote bag. She took out her notepad and pen as well. Maxine loved lists. She had decided she would make herself a checklist of "Knowns and Unknowns".

Before Maxine began writing her checklist of what she knew, and what remained a mystery, she put on her headset. She could always find a song to relate to any given situation, at any given time. With this talent, she fancied that she could be a "Quiet Storm" radio DJ one day.

Music was very soothing to her. It would help dissipate some of her anger-not all of it, but hopefully for Ben and Dawn's sake, *some of it*. "What will be the soundtrack for this drama?" She thought to herself. Mario fit her mood the best at the moment. She was glad she had recently downloaded his classic CD. He was young, but *his lyrics spoke like a man*.

She cued him up. The first track gave her hope, that somebody, someday, would love her better. "Damn right I am the kind of woman that deserves good things!" Maxine exclaimed aloud and wistfully.

Another track equally fitting to her situation, came on. The fact that he "couldn't say no" got her all riled up again thinking that cheating bastard Ben, would rationalize his cheating in the same way.

"Act a fool?" Maxine sat indignantly in her feelings. "Hell yeah, I'mma act a fool! I got a right to." She said to herself as another of his spot-on tunes filled her ears and soothed her soul.

"Yep, I found you out, Ben. Go ahead and pack-it up!" Maxine was seriously in her feelings now, but she managed a smile. Music could provide such levity in a situation. Just change "him" to "her" or vice versa, and it was instantly relatable.

By the time the music had finished understanding her, empathizing with her, telling her things were bad, that they would be all right, and finally concluding that it did not know what to do either, Maxine had made quite a list.

She'd titled her list: "What Dumbass doesn't know, I know":

#1: I know he is cheating (Now keep in mind, had he been honest with her, it wouldn't have been cheating. They could have come to an "understanding" However, he lied about it, and that is the action that said so much.)

#2: I know her name.

#3: I know where she works and lives.

#4: I know about her household relationships. (Thanks Ben!)

Maxine the Queen Blogger Plays Chess

#5: I know that I would not be the only one to be disappointed, or shall we say, *furious* to find out about this relationship.

#6: I can forward the emails to her job and possibly get her fired or threaten to (insurance).

#7: I'm glad that I transferred my money out of our joint account. (check)

#8: I have access to all of Ben's accounts. (smile)

#9: Ben doesn't even have access to all of his accounts. (laugh)

#10: Ben has no access whatsoever to my accounts. (laugh harder)

#11: The only thing that concerns Ben is money and good credit.

#12: I have the power to ruin both. (laughs even harder)

#13: The house is in my name. (Oh yes, she had learned a lot from "Exhale")

#14: An uncomfortable situation has been created for me.

#15: Options have been created for me.

#16: There will be get-back.

#17: Things may or will get ugly. (Ben will decide that)

#18: I can make it without Ben.

#19: I can find someone new. (easily)

#20: It may not be that easy for me to find someone new in this town.

#21: I might have to move.

#22: I don't want to find someone new. (Or, do I? Hmmm...)

#23: "Anonymous" was right. I have the upper-hand. I have knowledge. I have power. For every action the

Maxine the Queen Blogger Plays Chess

2 of them have taken together, I will make sure there
is an effective ripple-effect-reaction from me.

#24: Hell, hath no fury like a woman scorned.

#25: Ben isn't worth it. What we have is worth it.
(Or is it?)

#26: I might hurt more than Ben and Dawn with my
get-back. (They didn't care who they hurt. Why
should I care?)

#27: I am turning into someone I no longer know. (I
kinda like her)

#28: Am I turning into someone I don't want to know?
(Or, someone I want to be?)

Though Ben and Dawn had planned to keep her out of the
loop, Maxine had more information than either of them had.
As importantly, she had more information than either of
them *knew* she had.

Maxine would use the information to question Ben to see if
he would tell her the truth. If he lied, she would know, but
he wouldn't know that she already knew the truth. His lies
wouldn't pass her lie-detector test, and they would further
sink him.

She had been the victim of plenty of sucker-punches in her
day-- not just from Ben--but other men as well. She'd been
through worse from lesser men. Yep, unfortunately, Maxine
had, had many opportunities to hit someone back where it
hurt.

With that said, Maxine had never been a vindictive person.
She always took the high road. Those suckers only served to
make her stronger and more emotionally controlled.

Maxine the Queen Blogger Plays Chess

Vindictive was not something that she ever wanted to be but, being this kind of hurt, brings out so many unfamiliar characteristics in a person.

A person can be driven to want to do things to make the one(s) that hurt her, hurt just as much. Even if that was an impossible task, some might still try.

She thought that her reasoning nature had served her well in other circumstances, but sometimes enough was enough.

Sometimes, it was the infliction of emotional pain or physical pain that did the trick. Other times it was financial pain. Sometimes, it was humiliation. Sometimes, one would have to settle for just plain old *inconvenience* doing the trick.

Could Maxine be one of those people, so bent on getting even, that she would fundamentally change who she was to do it? She knew that once changed; she might never go back.

Was a betrayal by a genial but ultimately weak man like Ben worth it? A nagging question. A long time ago, she would have thought "Definitely", but now she thought "Definitely not." Would it feel good to ruin someone, or at least make them *think* she would? "Oh yeah," she said aloud. "It certainly would."

Maxine was not sure she how low she would go though. She wanted her blessings to continue to come. She thought Karma would certainly appear somewhere in the mix, if she changed substantially changed the nature of who she was and what she stood for.

Maxine the Queen Blogger Plays Chess

Having an extraordinary sense-of-self, and being the intuitive person that she was, Maxine processed things finitely. She was analytical. Yet, she was spontaneous. She was carefree. Yet, she was cautious.

She was a good person. She was torn by whether to stay that way *or not*. She was also not convinced that a get-back would necessarily take her out of the realm of reasonable. She was not so sure it would make her a bad person.

Maxine was definitely not a violent person. In fact, she'd never been in a physical fight in her life. However, she could verbally joust with the best of them. Her ability to keep calm and maintain diplomacy while being pointed in her choice of words, was legendary. Once someone had realized the depth of her verbal chastisement, it stuck with him or her.

Maxine was also the type though, that would fiercely protect what was hers, and she would make it very clear that there were few lengths that she wouldn't go to, to do so. Anyone wanting to tangle with her or hers, should do so, knowing it was at their own peril.

Fortunately for Maxine, she didn't have too many of those situations.

Maxine had been floored these last few days, but she would wait to see what her night would bring before she took any more action. If she could take anymore that is. She asked the ancestors for guidance.

Maxine arrived home and turned on the television to try to give her mind a break. She couldn't concentrate, but the TV provided her with some comforting background noise.

Maxine the Queen Blogger Plays Chess

She looked around the empty house that she'd been so excited to move into and fix-up. The uncertainty that hung in the air now, was palpable and uncomfortable.

Again, she thought that Ben would come home directly after work, considering the circumstances. Again, he did not. Maxine could see that Ben had planned to prolong a serious conversation for as long as he could. Not a very wise move on his part.

Some may even consider his delaying tactics as adding fuel to Maxine's fire. Ben knew Maxine was an introvert. He should know better than to give her time to think of a fitting verbal argument. "Oh, Ben." Maxine inhaled, "You're so out of your depth!"

She went upstairs to her computer and wrote for a long time. By the time she had taken a break, she had written, but did not upload blog entries, *"The Tea"* parts #6-9.

"The Tea" Day 3, Part 10:
"Ben"

Maxine the Queen Blogger Plays Chess

Maxine's imagination and pensive nature were two of her greatest assets, but at times those assets only served to keep her mind spinning. That is what her mind proceeded to do that evening as she waited for Ben to come home.

Ben was obviously in "deny, deny, deny" mode, so of course, to this point, truthful information hadn't been forthcoming from him. Without more first-hand information to add to the intel she'd already gathered, she would have to fill in the gaps with information she knew about Ben.

Maxine started to think about who Ben really was, or who she thought he was. Although, now she wasn't as certain, when push came to shove, she believed she knew what kind of man Ben was. She believed he was not stupid enough to blow all that he had worked for. *That they had worked for.*

Then again, he was a man. Did he think about those things? In a nutshell, Ben could be summed up by his financial astuteness, wit, looks, and his desire for punanny. He had the first 3 in abundance. Thus, he had no problems getting the latter-especially since he wasn't selective-outside of Maxine. **Of course.**

Maxine had to admit that even though this was the case, Ben had restrained himself pretty-well for most of their relationship. Maybe, even better than she had. *Ok, definitely better than she had.* The difference though was that Maxine had a higher standard for her dalliances than Ben did. Ben had at one time met her standards.

When it came to matters of the heart, Ben showed his love through monetary offerings. He didn't fall in love easily, but he was the type that could live with someone he didn't like.

Maxine the Queen Blogger Plays Chess

He was appreciative that he actually did love Maxine. Yet, Maxine felt it wasn't love that sustained Ben, it was more a fear of being alone that had really driven his side of the relationship.

Ben didn't like being alone and would attach himself to someone just so that he wouldn't be. To date, he'd been very lucky that no one had taken advantage of the fact that Ben was actually pretty malleable.

In the wrong hands, he could take easily be taken advantage of. Ben just wasn't the type to "man-up" and leave a relationship that no longer satisfied him.

If he could, Ben would prefer to keep Maxine around as a convenient out so that the women he cheated with wouldn't get too comfortable or expect too much from him.

Ben mostly went for the simple pleasures in life and avoided complications, like a plague. She thought about what kind of lover he was. He was the awkward kind.

While he had charm, he was not what one would consider "Suave". Not quite to stereotype though, was the fact that Ben loved to eat south-of-the-border and get freaky-*real freaky. He was a door opener.*

Ben had opened some doors mentally and physically for Maxine. Those doors would never be closed again. Damn, did he open some doors!

Maxine continued to torture herself in the hours that she waited for Ben to come home. She wondered if he'd gotten even a whisper of freaky with Dawn, as he had been with her. She also wondered if that was what he was doing now.

Dawn's emails indicated that Ben had rocked her sexual-world. Though, if she was a novice, she probably didn't know the half. Maxine knew Ben's kinda freaky, took time. Time was something that she could tell by their correspondence that they hadn't had enough of-*yet*.

Then again, knowing their time was limited and sporadic, and given the information provided in the letter and emails, maybe Ben and Dawn got right down to it. Maybe that was why Ben liked Dawn. She made it easy for him. Maxine could just imagine them laying-up in some hotel room at that very moment.

Oh, yeah, she could just see it. They would stop and get something to eat, take it up to the room, or order room service. They would have alcohol. Something Ben was rarely without.

Ben would kiss Dawn awkwardly, but excitedly with his firm lips. Well, really, his lips were just plain hard. He would then immediately go for feeling up her breasts.

Ben wasn't a breast man, but he would do the obligatory unbuttoning of Dawn's shirt and suck on hers. He would fake it for as little amount of time as possible. He would suck so lightly that Dawn would barely feel it, *but she would moan as if was the best sensation she'd ever had.*

He would suck them, nothing like the way Michael sucked Maxine's breasts. Michael did it so well, she would nearly orgasm from it. The way *he* explored her body before sex, was like sex itself. S*he was digressing.*

Maxine could not think about Michael right now for two reasons. One, she would remember the things he did to her, and she would start to feel good. And two, she would come face-to-face with her own deeds.

Her anger would begin to dissipate. Maxine was ready to be less angry, but she was not ready to not be angry at all. "Tssk, please!" She thought. "Besides," she told herself, "at least Ben knew when I was doing my business. He knew when, where and with who, (well, he knows the man I see most often anyway)."

If Ben needed to, he could reach Maxine anytime. He could even ask her not to go. Those courtesies, however small, let both Ben and Michael know, that Ben came first with Maxine. Knowing the deal gave Ben power over Michael. Maxine was there with Ben's permission, *not despite it.*

Maxine did not have the benefit of such information, courtesy, or power. Therefore, she was at a disadvantage (*maybe her only disadvantage*), and thus, she was hopping mad! She channeled her anger back into focus.

Ben would then reach into Dawn's panties and stroke her punanny with his thick fingers. They would move over to the bed, and he would take her panties down and proceed down South with his mouth.

He may stop mid-eating and turn on a porn flick. Then he would get back to it and do a fairly good job at it.

Maxine the Queen Blogger Plays Chess

He might attempt to kiss her softly across her thighs and up and around her torso, but he wouldn't linger there sucking on her flesh until he left a mark. Ben was not an all-points man.

He would go where he knew there was a sensation to get the job done easily and quickly, rather than explore for unexpected places of sensation.

Or, maybe, he was only like that with Maxine…*hmmm…another reason to be mad, if that was the case.* After Dawn came, he would hold his still rock-hard dick in his hand and ask with a smile "Did you like that?"

Dawn, of course, would say "Yes" because she did like it, and because she wanted to affirm Ben. Even if Dawn were dissatisfied, she would not say so, because that is something *Maxine* would do.

Dawn had to be different from Maxine, otherwise, why would Ben step out on her? She had to find ways make herself better than Maxine-or at least make Ben think she was. *Even though Dawn was not even close.*

Dawn would then reach for Ben's dick and blow him like her life depended on it. She would look up at him and watch him enjoying the sensations and suck harder.

Then, they would sit up and talk and eat the food they'd gotten. Ben would spin some fantasy about how complicated his life had become lately.

As part of his small-talk, Ben would reveal his business, and *Maxine's business* as well. He would talk about how bored he was, how hard he worked. Of course, he would never mention that he was not bringing anything to the table to engage Maxine.

He would talk about Maxine's flaws, *and never reflect on his own.* In the moment, he would say just enough to make Dawn feel that she could give him what he needed.

Dawn would let him know that she would make herself readily available to him now and in his future moments of need.

"The Tea" Day 3, Part 11:
"Dawn"

Maxine the Queen Blogger Plays Chess

When it came to Dawn, Maxine had to think of two different Dawns. A younger version, and an older version. She thought, both an older and younger Dawn would lie in bed and tell Ben her struggles, her hopes, and her ambitions. She would try to seem like she had it going on, was on-the-move-*you know, doing things and going places!*

She would talk too much, thinking that she was "sharing" and being "open" with Ben. She would think, that she made Ben think, he was getting to see a side of her, that her husband didn't get to see.

She would make herself seem like she was mysterious, rather than admit, her husband was no longer interested in "seeing" her. Dawn would suffer from TMIS-Too Much Information Syndrome. She would not realize that Ben did not care for all that "sharing" and "open" kind of stuff.

She would subtly pry him for more information about Maxine. She would keep a mental-checklist of the things that seemed to bother Ben about Maxine. Dawn would make sure she did not do any of those things.

Dawn would keep a mental-checklist of the things that he favored about Maxine and *try to adopt similar traits.* She would sympathize with how hard his life was at home. She would demonstrate her understanding in the ways that he looked for.

An older or younger Dawn, would make Ben feel that his love was the best love she'd had in a long time, *or ever.* When he would touch her, she would moan appropriately. She would *reciprocate* appropriately.

Maxine the Queen Blogger Plays Chess

An older Dawn would become more flexible, more conscious of stray, not-supposed-to-be-there hairs. She would be more sexual then she had been in a long time, or ever.

She would be buck-wild partly because that was a fun state to be in, but mostly, because she knew he would like that. Young or old, Dawn would make Ben feel that being with *her* was the most comfortable and easiest it could be to be with a woman.

If Ben wanted adventure, Dawn would be adventurous. If Ben wanted a freak, Dawn would be his freak. If Ben wanted an ear, Dawn had two. Dawn would be his sanctuary. She would give Ben his escape from *the harsh realities of a real relationship*.

If Dawn were older, when Ben could use sage advice from an elder...*she could give him that too*. If she were older, they would be equal partners in Dawn's mind. She would think (as Ben did) that there are not many men out there like him. Yet, she would also have her own shit together.

If she were older than Ben, she would be over 50. She *should* have her shit together by then. Dawn and Maxine might be on a level playing ground on that one. *Because, Maxine definitely had her shit together*.

Maxine added to her imaginary profile of Dawn. Dawn would do whatever she needed to do, to make sure Ben hung around. After all, she wasn't getting any younger. If Dawn were older, she would make sure she wore nice lingerie and smelled good all the time. She would make sure that no hair (on her head, or elsewhere) was out of place.

Maxine the Queen Blogger Plays Chess

Dawn would wear things and do things, that Ben would like and enjoy. When you're younger, and your body is naturally on-point, you can get away with mis-matched undies. Dishelved bed-head *outside of bed was still considered sexy*, when you're young, When you're older, you have to draw attention elsewhere.

Dawn would bend her bones in ways that would get her the compliments she needed to boost her ego. She would kid herself into believing she could hang with the best of the younger girls. "That isn't likely, but it's not impossible." Maxine charitably gave her.

Dawn would miraculously do all kinds of things she had never done before, to show she had something to offer that Ben would want (hopefully).

If she were older, Dawn would look at herself in the mirror and try to figure out ways to make herself look younger and attractive. She would read-up on how to make her punanny tighter.

She would buy "sexy" clothing and hope that on her...they were still sexy *and* that they made her sexy too. Dawn would look as good as she could, with what she had to work with. She would wonder if what she had to work with was enough for Ben.

Dawn would be or do things she probably had not been or done in a long time *if ever, for anyone*. She would say to herself, "It has been too long!" She would begin to feel that she was getting her life back on track.

Maxine the Queen Blogger Plays Chess

An older Dawn would try to play-up, that "older woman" advantage of having been around the block a few times. She'd play-up having learned a few tricks. At the same, she would play-down that she'd done a few tricks in her heyday.

She would play-down the "older woman" aspect when it was not such an advantage, particularly when it came to Maxine's youth and natural beauty.

If Dawn were older, she would get used to the attention Ben gave her. She would begin to crave it too much. She would only see Ben's good traits, his generous side, his stable side, his accomplished side, his smart side, his monetary finesse, and his freaky side.

She would judge whether he was the type to pay for plane tickets, hotel rooms, nice restaurants and weekend adventures away and not just pay for rooms for a few hours the next town over.

She would be happy with little things and anticipate the big things to come. Dawn could tell Ben had pretty good taste and didn't skimp. She would like that. She'd like being the recipient of his kindness (and not realize it was just a stringing-along tactic Ben was quite good at using).

If Dawn were younger or older, she would not pressure Ben but would indicate her feelings of physical need for him (nothing about what he could offer her materially-not yet). She would do what she could to prolong that wooing phase.

If Dawn were younger, she would use Ben for what she couldn't obtain for herself. She would tell herself that she was giving him what he needed in exchange. She would tell herself that Ben was with her because she was "special" and because she was "different."

If she were older, she would become emotionally attached to the physical attention he gave her. She would do everything, and be everything for Ben, that she was not doing for or being with her husband.

Even if she wasn't particularly keen on an idea, if Dawn were older, she wouldn't say "No" to Ben, because she wanted to do what he needed and be what he needed her to be. She would convey to him that their time together was "important" and "special" to her. She would slowly try to make herself a priority.

She would become disappointed when she didn't get the time she would begin to feel she deserved. She would turn into the "older" version of the desperate housewife.

She would try to make Ben feel that her demands on his time were reasonable. It was his fault, she'd stroke his ego. After all, the demands were a result of the insatiable hunger *he* had created in her. Ben would like that she was insatiable for him, but he would tire of the expectations on his time.

Dawn would think that if things went South for her and her husband, she would have Ben to rely on. *But, Ben would be busy keeping his own house in order.*

In her mind, Ben would make Dawn feel powerful and important. "Why else would he risk so much to be with her?" She'd think. Just as most "other" women, young or old, arrogantly wanted to, Dawn would believe Ben's every lie and line.

Maxine the Queen Blogger Plays Chess

Dawn would just be plain stupid to risk so much to be with Ben. *Maxine would make sure that aspect did eventually "dawn" on her.*

Whatever age Dawn was, Ben would allow her to have that power-*in her own mind.* He would call her "Sexy" and "Hot" because he knew she needed to hear it. Ben knew that Dawn was quite desperate to hear it.

Regardless of age, what woman doesn't want to hear that she's sexy and hot? He would allow Dawn to feel that she had something over Maxine. Ben would make Dawn believe that she was some-kind-of-woman, *to be wanted by him.*

At whatever age she was, Dawn would learn to push away thoughts of what Ben and Maxine were doing, when he wasn't with her. She would also push away thoughts of what, perhaps he was doing- with someone else altogether.

Dawn would believe him when he told her that he and Maxine didn't do the things that the two of them did together. Dawn would push doubts away when Ben made excuse after excuse of why he could not see her time, after time.

Dawn would tell herself that if Maxine and Ben were doing anything, he was probably thinking of her. Maybe he was. Maybe he wasn't. Maybe that was an unknown for Maxine, but certainly, it was an unknown for Dawn.

Dawn would look for advantages such as age, weight, education, accomplishment, eyes, and lips. Whatever she thought she could find an advantage in, she would claim it. She would compare and contrast everything. She would home in on every mention of Maxine, and judge how much and if, and why, he still cared enough for Maxine to stay with her.

She would come to realize that she wasn't superior, just a convenient lay. If she were an older woman, in her mind, and in Ben's, she would know that even if you're an older woman who is still hot, when push comes to shove, at the end of the day, compared to Maxine…she'd still just be the *old* in older.

She might be just a few years older than Ben, but that would make her quite a few years older than Maxine. She would try to make him forget about that, but wouldn't be able to escape in her mind, that men paid attention to those things.

If she were a younger woman, she would be threatened by such a long relationship, and two lives so intertwined. However, her momentary feelings of power would convince her that Ben was hers, and she had something to offer him that Maxine didn't, couldn't or wouldn't.

Dawn would manipulate Ben's thoughts in such a way as to be seen as supportive. She would be understanding of him, read him for the type of reaction he wanted. Did he need someone to be outraged at Maxine's supposed gall? Or, did he want someone to be objective, and even sympathetic toward Maxine?

If Dawn was young, would she be sophisticated enough to make split-second decisions as to what Ben needed from her in the moment? Would she be able to cement for him that she could understand him?

Maxine the Queen Blogger Plays Chess

Would Ben buy the story she was spinning about her ability to relate, and her ability to just listen?

Youth. For man or woman, was that one aspect of life, that no matter how hard one tried, could never be bought-only lived vicariously through.

Maxine looked considerably younger than her age and was certainly much younger than 50, even 40. She was youthful but wouldn't consider herself "young". Hmmm, could be an advantage for Dawn...*if, she was young*.

Right now, though, a younger or older Dawn would not think about how Maxine could make her real-life house-of-cards come crashing down. Instead, she would focus on the fantasy and continue to rearrange her life to get some of Ben's attention and whatever else he had.

Dawn would think that she was "acting normal" to those around her. She would get too excited, get too overconfident, and get *way, waaaay* ahead of herself.

Dawn would mess-up big time. It would be too late when she realized that she was *way, waaaay* out of her league.

Maxine the Queen Blogger Plays Chess

"The Tea" Day 3, Part 12:
"The Quandary"

Maxine the Queen Blogger Plays Chess

As Maxine envisioned Ben and Dawn lounging around in bed, drinking beer or wine, she imagined Ben would be thinking about how much easier that was than to face Maxine.

He would think it more fun to find someone who would find his old stories new and his old jokes funny. He would think about how much easier that is, than it is to work on himself, or with Maxine to at least try to make things right between them.

Everything with Dawn would be new for a while-even if she was old. That would keep Ben going until he tired of her and was ready to jet. He would talk about his long-range plans, and possibly include her in them *just enough* to give her hope that she had something real with him.

As long as Maxine stayed around and because Dawn had a husband, Ben would always have an out for himself. At first, he would only think with his dick, and about all the advantages he had with Dawn. He would focus on all the fun they could have, and all the stress-relief she could bring him.

The newness of their relationship would temporarily hide several facts. Dawn would not realize that Ben was thinking "There must be something about her that is not fulfilling her husband's needs; otherwise, she wouldn't be here with me."

Ben would think Dawn was at fault because, in his mind, it was never a man's issues at issue.

Ben would think about why it was, that Dawn's husband just was not into her anymore. He knew that there were two sides to every story. She may say one thing, but what was the other side of the story? He would be watching her closely for the side of the story that Dawn wasn't telling.

Ben would start to scrutinize Dawn's looks and decide she did not have natural beauty. Her looks were all smoke and mirrors. He would think, "I mean, she's no looker, but she probably never was. So, that can't be a factor in why her husband was no longer interested in her."

Dawn may be thinner here, and tauter there, but she wasn't really cute. Ben would silently note her flaws, but would point out only good things to her, to keep her hooked.

Maxine was naturally pretty and didn't have to wear make-up. Maxine exuded sex appeal; she just hadn't been giving-off any sex appeal of late. *To him anyway.*

Ben would secretly wonder if Dawn would eventually begin to nag him, as he believed every woman did. "Of course, she will." He'd decide. He would weigh the pros and cons of a relationship (he hesitated to call it that) with Dawn as opposed to his with Maxine.

He would think about Dawn in practical terms and figure out if a "relationship" with her would bring him the same advantages over their long-run, as his long-run with Maxine had.

Ben would think of the work it takes to start over, even with someone who would do whatever it takes to please him-*at least Dawn would for a little while.*

He would also think about his age and wonder if playing the

field was practical anymore. If he was to settle down again with someone new, could it be with Dawn?

Would Dawn get bored with him and vice versa? Did he still have it in him-what it took for a man to keep a woman? He was very good looking, and women flirted with him all the time.

There was one thing Ben did know. He knew that he would never find someone like Maxine ever again. So, even if he was not satisfied with her now, he knew that he wouldn't find anyone else he would be as happy with. He didn't want the headache of even trying.

Ben told himself that he was fulfilling a need for Dawn, better than her husband did. But silently he would think, "I ain't trying to be nobody's husband or a replacement for one."

He would think about all that. He would think about how easily he'd hooked Dawn. Ben would convince himself that indeed, "I've still got it." It felt good to still have it, even if Dawn was far from what one would call a difficult or enviable catch.

Ultimately, he would rationalize and chuck it all up to two people who have needs, and who are simply, harmlessly, fulfilling them. He needed fulfillment in an area that Maxine wasn't providing. That's all it was, nothing more, and nothing less.

Maxine would not understand, he'd rationalize. Ben knew that Maxine was the only woman he'd ever met who would at least try to understand. He knew that regardless of how mad

Maxine the Queen Blogger Plays Chess

Maxine got initially, she would eventually see the benefits for herself and allow him this "understanding."

Then again, Max saying that she understood, and that she was "Ok" with being flexible is one thing. Actually, being understanding and flexible is another. "Why take that chance?" Ben reasoned.

Ben knew that Maxine was actually pretty mild-mannered and low-to-no stress. It was difficult to find a woman like her. If he messed this up, at his age, he could find himself in a world of hurt if forced to find someone else to be his companion.

Women didn't get any more flexible as they got older and he could get mixed up with someone who turns out to be a real witch. He shuddered at the thought.

It was best that Maxine did not know about this tryst, Ben concluded. Ben created (a much shorter) list in his mind, as to why:

#1: I don't want to lose Max- I really do love her, and I know she loves me no matter what shit we pull on each other. (I should tell Max)

#2: I do not want to jeopardize all that I've/we've built. (Better not say anything to Max)

#3: Maxine would get mad and give me shit about this and bring it up whenever it was convenient for her-unlike when she rendezvous, and I don't sweat it. But then again, at least she is honest with me about it. (I should tell her)

Maxine the Queen Blogger Plays Chess

#4: Maxine could complicate my living arrangements if provoked. Though I can take care of getting a new place, why suffer a headache? (Better not say anything to her)

#5: Dawn isn't important enough to go through drama. I just need her to think she is until I'm tired of her. (No reasons to say anything to Maxine then)

#6: I don't want to give Maxine any ammunition that could be used against me should things get ugly. (Yep, it's better not to say anything)

#7: I could easily find someone new, but I know she'll never be as cool as Maxine. I'm too old for years of stress and headaches. (Definitely don't like starting over. Definitely not going to say anything)

"The Tea" Day 3, Part 13:
"Wait Expectations"

Maxine the Queen Blogger Plays Chess

Ben and Dawn would talk about how they were just "existing" going through the motions day-to-day, pining for each other. Eventually, their discretion would wane, *and on that weekend told of in "The Letter", it had.*

Maxine knew that Dawn had much to lose too-credibility, husband, reputation, job, finances, house. Would Maxine's leaving Ben make it easier for them? Is that what he and Dawn wanted? Would Ben want to stay with Maxine, or would he gladly accept the chance to be with Dawn unencumbered?

Should Maxine do whatever it took to keep Ben? Should she resign herself to the fact that he was gone? Would she gladly kick him to the curb? Maxine knew that even with the bubble burst, Dawn would continue to imagine having Ben all to herself.

Dawn would think only about the good things, the happy-ending. Dawn would, like every "other woman" tell herself that she is the type of woman who would never let things get bad like Maxine did.

She would not reflect on her relationship with her husband to find her flaws; she would only find his. Then, she would think that there is some reason Ben is staying with Maxine and that maybe things were not all bad.

Then, Dawn might even think for a split second "Men are dogs, it doesn't matter if you feed them steak-they'll still go looking for the bone. Is Ben a dog too?" Dawn wondered. "Am I the bone?" she wondered with a sudden gut-wrench.

Maxine the Queen Blogger Plays Chess

If Ben wasn't a dog, then her husband wouldn't be one either, if he were to do the same thing-right? Dawn would know that logic was illogical. She would be hopping mad, to find herself in Maxine's circumstance. "But, Dawn would redirect herself, Maxine isn't going to find out because we're careful."

Maxine thought that perhaps a divorce for Dawn was already "in the works," as she'd alluded to in an email. What Maxine didn't know though, was if Dawn was divorcing because of Ben? Or, had her divorce been in the works before meeting him?   Maxine knew that eventually, Dawn would grow tired of playing the game.

At some point, Dawn would want to be herself, and would begin to weigh if "herself" is something Ben would like- gray-haired punanny and all? Dawn would get tired of trying to be his everything and would make demands on Ben to be more like the everything she had in mind for him to be-*for her*.

Dawn might even figure out that "their song" was the same song Ben had used with Teresa, Carol, Phillipa and so on and so on. Instead of giving "them something to talk about," they would soon have nothing to talk about.

Dawn would tire of Ben's snoring, god-awful smelling farts, and incessant talking about himself. She will get tired of the fact that everything came down to money for him.

She would get tired of feeling like a caged bird, whose wings he continually clipped with his negativity, and his lack of support for her dreams, and ambition.

She would get tired of his drinking habits. She would tire of the way he smelled- no reeked of alcohol from 6:30 pm until he went to bed. Dawn would tire of hearing that perpetual snap of a beer can being opened. She would tire of the beer cans overflowing in the trashcan.

She would be turned off by his sour breath and certainly be turned-off from wanting to kiss him. She would figure out that the only places he wanted "to take her out" to were bars. She would soon notice the fact that bar-hopping is the only thing that he considered "going out." She would begin to nag Ben.

Maxine imagined that Ben would tire of Dawn's nagging. He would look for someone who didn't nag him, rather than work on himself or with her to make things better. He would look for someone younger-like Maxine's age, old enough to have it going on, and young enough to get it on, but who also didn't have any expectations of a "relationship".

He would want to have fun and get buck-wild, which Dawn would be too old to do. Ben would look for someone who desired to be his everything again, or at least spread her legs and pretend for a little while.

Still, in the now, Dawn wanted him and he appeared to want her. Like most "other women" Dawn believed she was "different", so Ben would be different. If all else failed, she would get freaky with him, and spread her legs when he needed her to, to keep him. Because "Hey good sex is good sex." She'd say.

If Dawn were a thinking older woman, she would want to make sure her home-base was secured should things go South. In the long-run, self-preservation would certainly come before good sex and making Ben feel good. Dawn would prefer to continue feeling bad, unloved, and unsexy by her husband, as she had stated she felt in her emails, before she would be thrown out into the street by him.

Maxine wondered if Dawn would take any negatives about her that Ben relayed and magnify them for him, so that he felt justified and ready to make a move. Isn't that what other women do?

Would Dawn *want* Maxine to kick Ben to the curb and make him available to be all hers? Was Dawn ready for that kind of commitment? Was the excitement of being Ben's secret side-chick a large-part of his attraction to her and the deal she'd made to keep him?

Maxine thought these things and imagined what the two of them, silently thought them to themselves when they were together *and when they were apart.*

According to their emails, they even lamented how hard it was to be discreet in such a small town. Maxine felt sure that in the interim of not knowing how things would play out, Ben and Dawn would still plan their next rendezvous. They were just that arrogant.

There were so many unknowns, "ifs", "ands" and "buts" for all of them at the moment. They would all just have to wait and see.

In the midst of Maxine's detailed, over-imaginings of the situation, Ben called to tell her not to wait up for him. "Oh?" Maxine prompted. "Why not?" She asked. Ben hedged. "My team and I have to go into Philly to meet with a potential contractor. We'll probably, just have dinner there and get hotel rooms, since it we'll all be tired and won't want to drive."

"Ben, are you eff'ing serious? Do you expect me to believe that with all that's going on, this is a business meeting that just came up at the last minute?"

Ben answered, "It didn't just come up. We knew that we might have to make the trip. You and I haven't exactly been on speaking terms for me to give you a heads-up about the possibility Max."

"Don't call me Max!" She yelled into the phone. Maxine was hotttt! She was not endeared by Ben's term of endearment for her.

"Ben, Philly is only 3 hours away. If your ass is not back here tonight, you will find your stuff out on the curb in the morning!" Maxine hung-up without letting Ben respond.

"The Tea" Day 4, Part 14:
"The Crystal Ball Blog"

Maxine the Queen Blogger Plays Chess

Fueled by her anger, Maxine had stayed up the whole night writing posts that would update her readers on the day's events and her feelings about them. She was mentally exhausted, but she kept on writing, filling in her unknowns with her imagined but educated guesses.

She had written and saved blog-posts parts #10-12 by the time she flopped onto her sofa and fell asleep. She fully expected Ben to come home before day light. Which he did, but just barely.

She woke up when she heard his key in the door at 3am. She raced to her computer and pressed publish for blog entries "*The Tea*" parts #6-9 and shut-down her computer. She would let them chew on those posts later that day. If Ben thought she was playing, he wouldn't think so after reading them.

She'd barely managed to put her external drive back into the vase before he reached the landing at the top of the stairs.

He stuck his head into her office and asked, "What are you still doing up? Don't you have to be to work in a few hours?" Maxine glared at him and said, "I was just about to start packing up your shit." She then closed her office door, laid down on the sofa-bed and fell right back to sleep from the sheer exhaustion of it all.

It would not be long before Ben and Dawn realized how much they had overestimated themselves, and underestimated Maxine. *Well, it would be too long for Maxine's satisfaction. But, not nearly long enough for theirs.*

That morning Maxine woke up tired. "Phew! It's hard work

thinking for four people--Ben, a younger Dawn, an older Dawn, and myself." Maxine thought, "I'm going to have to find out who and what I'm dealing with-or rather, who is going to be dealing with me!"

Then again, after all that thinking, she was so tempted to simplify things, and chuck it up to the fact that men didn't think that much. Most just did the basics to get laid. Knowing Ben, Dawn was someone who probably did not require a lot of strategy.

From the content of her emails, Maxine already had proof that Dawn didn't think that much. Maybe, Maxine was giving them too much credit.

Maxine understood that part of loving someone is accepting their faults as well as, their strengths, and believing that they would do the same for you. Were she and Ben at a point where their faults had become intolerable to each other?

Would Dawn "accept" Ben better than Maxine had of late? Maybe, things were to a point now, where she would. Maxine was quickly reaching the mode of not caring.

But…sometimes, Maxine thought too much about the deeper meaning of things. Then, on the rare occasion, she did not think enough. How was she to know which time this was? Where was the balance?

"If only I had a crystal ball!" Maxine thought. Then, she thought about her blog-really thought about it, in a new light. Her new way of looking at it, brought much more clarity than she had first believed it would.

Maxine the Queen Blogger Plays Chess

She readied for work where she would have more time to think about her new course of action. She left the house without telling Ben "Bye".

"The Tea" Day 4, Part 15:
"The Laugh"

Maxine the Queen Blogger Plays Chess

By the evening of Day 4 had rolled around, Ben had a little more time to think about what his life would be like without Maxine.

More immediately, he had time to think about what his life would be like *with* her, if she remained in a state of uncertainty. If nothing else, Ben knew that Maxine did not like being uncertain.

Ben also had time to read her updated blog to find out that Maxine had withdrawn $30,000.00 from their bank account. She was sure he wasn't prepared for "The Letter" "The Phone Call" "The Waiting Game" and "Maxine's Money" entries.

Maxine was quite sure that both Ben and Dawn were surprised and scared by just how much she knew about Dawn. Maxine was quite certain that they didn't realize that Maxine was hardly wringing her hands and sitting idly by waiting for Ben to inform her moves. On the contrary, she would now be strategically dictating theirs.

To let Ben and Dawn sit with her blog-entries for a while, she arrived home later that evening than usual. She was barely through the front door before Ben demanded, "Where's the money from my account!?"

She dropped her bag on the couch and walked casually past him toward the kitchen. She corrected him. "You mean *our* account." As she opened the cabinet for a wine class, she coolly said, "It's *my* money."

"That was my money!" Ben fired back.

Maxine the Queen Blogger Plays Chess

"Welp," Maxine quipped, and continued. "The checks were written in *my* name. I deposited them into *our* account, so you would have a tough time convincing anyone that it was *your* money. Besides, I only took out what I put in."

"You didn't put $30,000.00 in!" Ben shouted. *Ben was hotttttt!* "Well, see, what I meant was, I only took out what I put in...during the life of our relationship." Ben was speechless.

Ben was on fire! Ben was the type to get verbally angry, but he was not the physically violent type. He was too much of a man (at least in that respect) for that. He exhaled slowly and finished it off with an exasperated and defeated sigh.

Maxine could tell that he had spent a long day with his mind racing. Now, he was the exhausted one, and Maxine was just getting started. Ben always had his mind on his money and his money on his mind, so it wasn't unusual for him to check his account balance frequently.

Well, *their* account balance. When he had gotten to the part in her blog about how she had gone to the bank, Maxine suspected that was what prompted him to check their account today. She laughed inside.

"When am I going to get my money back?" Ben demanded. "When am I going to get the truth?" Maxine demanded back. Maxine knew that protecting Dawn's identity and privacy would only go so far *for free*.

For Ben-*everything and everyone had a price, one just needed to have the right currency.* He would sell ole Dawn down the river if he thought it would get his hands on some green. Maxine was quite sure Dawn did not realize that about Ben.

Maxine the Queen Blogger Plays Chess

It did not cross Ben's mind that he had already handed over a substantial bit of information on a silver platter. Maxine had all that she needed to continue to make his life miserable.

Ben thought he could avoid telling Maxine the truth about his and Dawn's affair. However, after reading about himself and Dawn in Maxine's blog entries, he was beginning to understand that Maxine already knew much more than they had hoped.

Due to "The List" post, Ben now knew that Maxine had Dawn's home address. Ben wasn't sure if Dawn's husband was the violent type. If Maxine wanted to make trouble there for them, she very well could.

Fortunately for both he and Dawn, Ben also knew that no matter how pissed-off Maxine was, she was not the type to put someone's physical well-being in jeopardy. That was one of the things he liked most about her.

Maxine was able to put things in perspective. It did concern him though, that Maxine had a devious side. She could be cleverer than a fox if provoked.

Maxine had done the most important thing already though. She had hit Ben where it hurt him most-his wallet. All that Ben's half-truths had bought him was the knowledge, that money does not buy happiness.

However, by keeping it out someone's hands who thinks money can buy happiness, sure bought Maxine a great deal of satisfaction.

Maxine the Queen Blogger Plays Chess

After Ben had all day to think about it, he foolishly thought he could regain some of the upper hand by coming partially clean.

Ben thought that maybe, just maybe, if he told the truth, he would get some money back.

All day he waffled between thinking that if he confessed enough to *his* satisfaction, it would satisfy *her,* and he would get the money, and some peace back into the household.

Then he'd think, "Would the truth appease Maxine? Or, would the truth make her even angrier?" Ben wasn't sure what to do, but he sure wanted the money back in the bank.

It didn't cross Ben's mind that like the money, that how Maxine would handle the situation, was out of Ben's hands. He thought he still had some control of the situation.

"Oh, Ben." Maxine thought as she listened to his half-assed attempts at half-truths. She laughed long and hard when he wasn't around.

Maxine could tell her special brand of Chess was working and keeping Ben and Dawn unnerved. Ben would come home immediately after work each day and try to pry her for clues as to what she was thinking. He would try to act normal so as not to tip his hand, but he was really bad at being coy.

Maxine would get a chuckle out of how Ben would race home to be the first one to collect the mail, now that he knew how she found out about him and Dawn. If she got to the mail first, Ben would hang over her shoulder as she sorted it.

Maxine the Queen Blogger Plays Chess

He was checking snail mail as regularly as he was checking his email.

If they were out shopping and Maxine ran into an acquaintance, Ben wouldn't leave Maxine's side. Maxine observed how his ears would perk up. He would study the acquaintance trying to determine if she was "Anonymous".

With the weekend coming up, Maxine had arranged a spa-day for herself in the big city. She decided that everybody needed a rest. Maxine would give Ben and Dawn a rest, at the same time she took hers-*sort of*.

Maxine didn't like to keep her readers waiting because they had become engaged in the story (although for them, the anticipation was part of the fun). To satisfy them over the weekend, she scheduled blog entries "*The Tea*" parts #10-12 to be published.

Maxine enjoyed knowing that while she was out of their sight, they would be wondering if she was planning something, or worse-*doing something* that they'd find out after it was too late.

While she and Ben went their separate ways for the weekend, Ben made sure that whatever he planned, didn't happen until the mail had arrived on Saturday. Waiting for the letter-carrier, gave him time to read her posts.

By this time, Maxine had written blog entries "*The Tea*" parts #13-14. She decided to wait until the following Monday to publish them.

"The Tea" Day 7, Part 16:
"The Embarrassment"

Maxine the Queen Blogger Plays Chess

It was late on Sunday night when Ben chose to wrap-up the weekend by finally "confessing" to Maxine that he and Dawn had a phone sex thing going on.

"All it *was*, he said, was something exciting that we both looked forward to, to break up the monotony of our days."

He said it was nothing but some teasing and release of pent-up frustrations through flirting. "Yeah, we met for drinks once in a while, but nothing ever happened." He said.

Ben confessed to Maxine that Dawn was ugly and dumpy and that in her wildest dreams Dawn could never compare to, or compete with, Maxine. *Something Maxine already suspected but would verify for herself.*

In his run of supposed honesty, he continued by explaining to Maxine that men want something easy. He explained that pretty girls required work and even *deserved* more effort. With Dawn, he did not have to work; she was grateful for any attention.

He told Maxine that Dawn was easy and convenient. He told her that she was the type that guys looked for when they wanted to step outside a relationship for a bit without a hassle down the line.

"Wow." Maxine thought. "If only Dawn could hear her prince charming now." Maxine took pleasure in knowing that Dawn would hear Ben's philosophy on the matter of her looks soon-enough. All his new-found candor would definitely be going in a blog entry.

Maxine the Queen Blogger Plays Chess

Maxine continued to bait him. When she asked Ben about Dawn's sex life, something she'd mentioned in her emails to him, Ben told her that Dawn's husband hadn't touched her in three years.

"Well, if she's unattractive, it's no wonder," Maxine replied. "Why would you be the one to reduce yourself so low then? She asked.

Ben responded by asking Maxine if she expected him to spend his 40's only having sex twice a year? Maxine didn't say it, but she thought "What are you doing to make me want to have sex with you?"

Maxine had made some stimulating changes over the last year. She was always educating herself by taking interesting classes. She was the curious sort, so she would hop from one interest to another, absorbing information that gave her something to talk about, kept her interesting, kept her mind and her body busy.

She'd tried to share some of her interests and skills with Ben, but he never cared to indulge her. He never gave her credit for working as hard as she did to make their relationship interesting.

Everything was always about him. What *he* was doing, *his* plans (*well, some plans he had left out*), and *his* accomplishments. It was always about how *his* day was at work, and blah, blah, blah. To be fair though, Maxine understood that lack of giving credit was a fault they shared.

Instead of going on the attack, Maxine simply said: "No, I don't expect you to go through your 40's with it only two times a year. It appears though, that you haven't been getting it only two times a year."

Ben genuinely thought Maxine was a fool. The emails didn't lie. If they weren't having sex, oral or otherwise, then why would Dawn's period be an issue, a topic of conversation? Something that would take her of commission to make him have to "wait."

The nasty witch! Maxine exclaimed to herself as she thought about that particular email. Maxine so wanted to believe Ben was apologetic, but she was a thinking person. Two and two just weren't adding up to four.

"He'd better get the hell out of Dodge with that noise, and he'd better not come back until he had the truth to tell about the sex in his and Dawn's relationship." Maxine thought.

Dawn's unattractiveness she could believe, and knowing Ben, that wouldn't have stopped him if the getting was to be got. The balance of the scale was shifting again. Maxine was losing her patience with Ben. Dawn would pay for that.

Maxine was very aware that Dawn probably understood that the jig was up. The veil of secrecy had been lifted. Maxine wondered if Dawn was afraid. Was Dawn unsettled, as Maxine had been unsettled? Was she nervous and on edge, as Maxine had been on edge?

Did Dawn immediately go through her acquaintances to see which one she and Maxine had in common and who may have spilled Dawn's tea? Did Dawn look suspiciously at every woman? Did she look at every stranger and feel paranoid that her eyes lingered on her a bit longer than usual and then wonder if she was "Anonymous"?

Dawn would ask herself if she should she visit with Maxine and have a heart to heart. She wondered if an apology would appease Maxine. Then, she would correctly determine that a visit to her wouldn't be a good move.

She would wonder if Maxine would pay her a visit and have a heart to heart. Maybe. Dawn was deathly afraid that she would. She would get to work early every day to check that all was quiet on the J P Clarke and Bagger front.

If her boss or corporate office called her, would Dawn answer the call hesitantly, and with a trembling hand as she thought, "Oh Shit! Maxine's gone and done it! Maxine's taken this to my corporate headquarters to get me fired!"

Was Dawn planning moves at home to preempt anything that Maxine could dish out? Did she hope that Ben could quell the fire inside Maxine? Maxine was pretty sure that Dawn was praying she would just chill. *Dawn's best option by far was to hope that Maxine was more considerate to her than she and Ben had been to Maxine.*

Were Ben and Dawn planning their own CYA (Cover Your Ass) countermeasures to refute anything Maxine could prove? Dawn had to know that Ben was certainly making attempts to quell the fire inside Maxine.

Would Maxine believe that they were honest attempts, after being lied to over and over? Would Ben and Maxine try to make things right between them? Even if Maxine chilled with Ben, would Maxine chill with her? Maxine didn't have any obligation to her.

Maxine the Queen Blogger Plays Chess

Did Dawn really believe she deserved to be spared any heartache? Had she spared Maxine any? Would it matter that she tried to be discreet? *No, it probably wouldn't.*

Maybe like Maxine, Dawn had become quite alert, and an information hound. But if she had, what could she do with any information that she might dig up, that wouldn't further bring on Maxine's wrath?

Did Dawn think, "Well, maybe if I tried to do something to keep her in check, I could do it anonymously..." and then she'd quickly think, "No, Maxine would without a doubt know that she was this particular "Anonymous" and she would know where to find her.

It was highly unlikely that Maxine wouldn't go smooth-off, if Dawn tried some damage control measures like that. No, if she tried some shit like that, Dawn would definitely tip the scales to the side of Maxine's wrath.

There would be absolutely no "chilling" from her to be hoped for then. "Damn!" Dawn thought. Maxine had her in an awkward position. Maxine could ruin everything she'd worked for by dropping a dime to her husband- or her job. Or both.

Dawn thought that she'd better be careful. She would let Ben handle Maxine. Dawn would hope like hell Ben could.

Maxine's used her blog to cleverly drive a wedge between Dawn and Ben. At the same time, they worked together-reluctantly by trying to strategize how they could cover their tracks. One false move though, and they could blow the whole sordid affair wide open (*or force Maxine to*) to their own detriment. So, wouldn't it be better for them to just chill with any thoughts of trying to outwit Maxine?

Ben's supposed confession the night before had cemented for Maxine that he was and always will be as spineless as a jellyfish. As she listened to him spew his lies, she understood that she did not come first with him. Ben was only looking out for himself.

Maxine understood that even though he was lying as a means to keep her, he didn't understand that honesty was the only way he could.

So, fresh from a relaxing and informative weekend, Maxine thought it was now time to strike Dawn where it hurt *her* most. Nobody really likes Mondays anyway, so to keep Dawn and Ben on their toes and give them a little more shock to their systems, Maxine chose that day to pay Dawn a visit--*at her job*.

Maxine was even kind enough to bring her a bouquet of nearly dead flowers with a pre-printed card that simply read "Thinking of you."

When she got to Dawn's office and asked for her by her name, a co-worker gave Maxine a strange look. The colleague asked her to "Wait here please." Then, she went to the back where Dawn was. Maxine could hear her tell Dawn, "I think Maxine is here for you".

"Interesting." Maxine thought. Was the colleague warned that Maxine might possibly appear at her job? Should Maxine be worried about Security approaching her? Or, was this a

Maxine the Queen Blogger Plays Chess

colleague-friend of Dawn's and thus, privy to Dawn and Ben's affair? By extension, she knew who Maxine was?

She told Dawn that Maxine was here, without Maxine giving her name. "So, it seems Dawn is a blabber-mouth like Ben. Hmm, they have that in common." Maxine thought.

"That might mean that this chick reads my blog too." Maxine thought. She smiled, then frowned. On one-hand, she hoped Dawn's colleague was tuning in to her blog for the latest.

That would mean that not only had Maxine blown-up Ben and Dawn's charade with each other, but she'd also let their friends in on it.

Then, again, it also meant that the two just couldn't keep Maxine's name and game out of their sordid business. Maxine really hated when people had to use other people's lives to make their own lives interesting!

"Oh well!" Maxine quietly whispered as she waited. Dawn's embarrassment factor was sure to be off the register by now, knowing that her friends now knew what Ben really thought of Dawn. Maxine imagined her new reality was surely contrary to the fantasy Dawn had spun about Ben to her friends.

"They didn't plan on it being me that would give them something to talk about!" Maxine smirked, as she recalled another email where Ben and Dawn referenced their "cheat" song. The only thing that would send Dawn's embarrassment off the charts was if Dawn's husband found out.

Maxine the Queen Blogger Plays Chess

When Dawn timidly came to the front-desk where Maxine was waiting patiently, Maxine could immediately see the look of recognition flash in her eyes.

Though they'd never met, Dawn knew who Maxine was based on Ben's description. Well, she knew what Maxine looked like anyway. Maxine was quite sure if Dawn "knew" her, she would never have gotten involved with Ben to begin with.

Maxine confirmed that Ben had at least been telling the truth that this chick was no show-stopper. Dawn was, exhausted-*and she looked it.* Dawn's stringy hair with fried-ends, seem to be on edge right along with her nerves.

"Damn!" Maxine thought upon first-glance of the hot-mess in front of her. "Ben, you gonna let yourself go out like that?"
"Yep, just goes to show, you give 'em steak, and they still go for the ratty-ass bone." Maxine thought.

By appearing at her job, Maxine had let Dawn know that she can tangle with Maxine and what was Maxine's, if she wanted to, but Dawn would surely regret it if she did.

Maxine wasn't intimidated by the very old and desperate housewife. Not one bit. Ben may have chosen the bone instead of the filet mignon, but that nasty business was on him. Whatever lies Ben would try to spin, he couldn't refute the evidence.

Maxine could not believe that Ben could sink that low. No real man with any self-respect should or would sink that low-no matter how easy the getting was. It says something about

Maxine the Queen Blogger Plays Chess

a man *(Ben)*, who settles for some*thing* (Dawn) nobody else *not even a man obligated by marriage, (Dawn's husband)* would want.

Maxine smirked as she handed Dawn the flowers and said "These are for you." Dawn asked snidely "Who are they from?" Maxine shrugged her shoulders and said, "Read the card," as she turned and left.

After finding out that Maxine was unafraid to let her know that Maxine will always be the Queen, in life and in this game of Chess, was Dawn tempted to confess to her husband?

After realizing that Maxine could and would show up at her job, was Dawn tempted to preemptively break up her own unhappy home, on the off chance that Maxine…*or someone else would try to?*

Should Dawn open up Pandora's Box for her husband, before Maxine did? What if Maxine never opened it? Dawn would cause a lot of heartache for herself for nothing.

Could Dawn rely on the lame defense of "only fantasies and flirtation" with her husband, more successfully than Ben was able to do with Maxine? Dawn was stressing over the mountain of unknowns.

Dawn began to seriously doubt that Ben was worth the discomfort that Maxine was bringing to her doorstep. She called Ben immediately after Maxine left.

Maxine was in complete disgust at what she had just seen. Before she could reach the parking-lot, get into her car to call Ben, and let him know how disgusted she was, Ben was blowing up her cell phone.

Maxine the Queen Blogger Plays Chess

"Max!" Ben implored, "What are you doing?!" He yelled when she finally answered. Then, he thought the better of his tone. "Can we keep this between you and me?" He asked with much more contrition.

Maxine noted the change in his approach. She calmly replied, "You shouldn't be worried about what I'm doing. You should be worried about *who* you are doing. That is one nasty looking witch. You're disgusting!" She then hung up the phone.

She was done. Maxine smiled to herself. She had put Dawn and Ben on their toes. She'd accomplished her mission.

With her next blog-posts, Dawn and Ben would finally see that Maxine had been playing them. She was in control of this Chess game of betrayal. Maxine almost hated to end the story with the big reveal that was coming.

Maxine was tired though. She wanted to move on. She needed to focus on how she would do that, as opposed to masterminding a psychological thriller.

Maxine went home and fired-up her computer. She published blog entries, "*The Tea*" parts #13-14.

"The Tea" Day 8, Part 17:
"The Read"

Maxine the Queen Blogger Plays Chess

Maxine had calmed down considerably over the last week, even to the point of indifference. Maxine smiled as she typed the final post on the story.

It was in her last post that she let Ben, Dawn, and anyone else they'd shared her blog with, in on her secret.

It was just by-chance, that several weeks prior to finding out about Ben's affair, that she had found out that Ben had discovered her blog. One day, she was on her computer and saw her blog address in the history of sites recently visited.

Maxine made sure to always clear her browser history. When she saw it listed as recently viewed, and she had not been online to write that day, she knew then, that Ben had been reading it.

She wasn't sure how he'd found it. As covert as she was about concealing the blog, she still must have left some evidence. Ben was not the blog-reading sort to have just coincidently stumbled upon it. She had wanted to keep it a secret from everyone-and especially from him.

Ben had unknowingly confirmed for Maxine that he was reading her blog. Sometimes, he'd make an awkward reference to a musing, she'd written about on her blog. Or, he would sing a song she might have referenced in a post.

Ben thought that because he was commenting on a public event or story, that Maxine would connect his comments to it, and not to her blog. However, Maxine knew his comments were too coincidental to be a coincidence.

Maxine the Queen Blogger Plays Chess

Other times, Ben would make more pointed comments hoping to bait her into asking him if he read her blog. Maxine was too big a fish to bite on such small bait. Plus, she did not want to give him the satisfaction of her knowing that he had discovered her blog-*and her secrets.*

Maxine preferred that Ben think she was clueless because, in his mind he didn't think she was picking-up on his hints. Maxine knew that when people think you are stupid or think you are not paying attention, they are more likely to play their hand.

So, she acted as if everything he hinted at, was new information to her. His comments only provided her more evidence that he indeed read her blog. Because Maxine ignored his hints, it made Ben all-the-more want her to know that he knew about the blog.

Yet, because Ben hadn't said anything directly to her about it, Maxine played along, but took his silence as an indication that he was spying on her. That intrusion into her privacy really ticked her off. Ben just wasn't the type that could let her have anything of her own, without inserting himself into the picture somehow.

What started out as an outlet for her because she was new to the area and friendless, had become a fun pasttime. She relished the privacy of being able to write out her thoughts and observations "Anonymously". She looked forward to having 'someone' she could talk to that was separate and apart from Ben.

Now, not only had had Ben taken her trust in him away, he had also stolen her and her blog's anonymity. He had essentially found her diary, shared it with friends and made it so she could never write "Anonymously" using that blog name again.

Ben knew that Maxine valued her privacy and guarded it zealously. While he was an extrovert who rarely held back with his business-except, obviously his affairs-she was much more guarded and reserved with hers.

Privacy was like a security blanket to Maxine. Ben had pulled the blanket out from under, from around and from over her. He had exposed so many sides of her. She would not forgive him for that. "Damn him!" Maxine said aloud to herself as she reflected on the last week.

Had Ben not been cheating, Maxine might have eventually told Ben about her Blog and put him out of his misery of trying to keep a secret. Boy, was Maxine glad that "The Letter" had come before she had a chance to do that!

Ben's arrogance and loose-lips would compel him to tell Maxine's business to Dawn. So, Maxine knew that Dawn was reading her blog as well.

Maxine was an observer and she didn't like knowing she was being watched. Ben's lack of respect for her privacy, showed a lack of loyalty to her.

Because Ben and Dawn were arrogant, they had thought themselves slick by essentially spying on Maxine and using her blog for pillow-talk.

Maxine the Queen Blogger Plays Chess

In some cases, Ben and Dawn would probably get-off on reading her erotic stories. The thought of them using them to fuel their rendezvous, just goaded Maxine.

They also thought that Maxine's blog would be fun to share with their friends. Ben and Dawn had been voyeurs into her life and adventures and had invited others to be as well.

That Ben wanted to share his business was one thing. Ben's business *apart from her* was his to tell. However, telling Maxine's business without her permission was an egregious over-step that was unforgivable in her world.

It was that lack of loyalty-on so many levels- that had hurt Maxine the most. In many of Maxine's locally inspired entries, Ben and Dawn could probably guess who it was in the sleepy little town that Maxine was writing about.

As it turned out, not revealing to Ben that she knew, that he knew about her blog, had served Maxine well when she found out he was cheating. "All praise to the ancestors!" Maxine thought. She was glad she hadn't immediately told him she knew. Waiting and thinking about it, as they had suggested had paid-off handsomely.

When Ben began to realize that his affair was the subject of one of Maxine's latest "locally inspired entries", it gave him further incentive to keep quiet about knowing about it.

While Maxine was ticked that he knew about the blog, that knowledge turned out to have given Maxine the upper-hand. Her anger had dissipated when she thought about how she could use his spying on her-against him.

Maxine the Queen Blogger Plays Chess

It was on that day that she'd wished for a crystal ball, that she'd had an epiphany. By giving herself some time to think, she was able to be proactive, rather than reactive.

Maxine didn't need a crystal ball to tell her what was going to happen after all. "Let's give them something to read about!" She thought then.

She realized that she didn't need to take-out femme-fatal style revenge. She might not be able to tell the future, but she could certainly *shape* her future with the help of some well-planted bait. Bait, that she could leave on her blog. Maxine was indeed, one lucky girl- *whatever the outcome.*

Maxine did have the upper hand. Her blog became not only her therapy, it also became her chess board from which she would direct the course of events. As in a strategic move in a game of chess, she would use her blog to "check" her mate *and his pawn.*

She smiled remembering the day there was a break in the clouds that showed her a new set of moves. Maxine was quite proud of her genius strategy.

While Ben was out gallivanting around town, she would valiantly pour out her heart to her readers in strategic doses. Her cleverness would spell Ben and Dawn's doom.

Maxine had been able to laugh as she typed the trail that *she* wanted them to follow. Being able to find humor in the situation definitely dulled her thoughts of other kinds of revenge.

Maxine the Queen Blogger Plays Chess

She laughed knowing that every single day, Ben, and Dawn would check her blog to plan their moves and lies based on her posts. She laughed knowing that they were on edge when she didn't post for a day or two. She laughed because they were so unsuspecting of Maxine's stealth.

Each time she wrote an entry and strategically posted it, Maxine laughed. They didn't know that she was planting what *she* wanted them to *think* she was thinking and planning.

Maxine laughed thinking about how Ben and Dawn thought they were the stealthy ones and could counter her moves. She laughed long and hard when she imagined the look on their faces when they realized she'd already made her move and that they'd played right into her hands.

Maxine had reversed their course as well. She had them in mate-check.

Now, Ben and Dawn were dazed and confused because of her blog. The blog no longer amused them. They were feeling quite embarrassed. What had been a private affair between them and something to snicker behind Maxine's back about, was suddenly very public in a small town that had plenty of gossips.

They had used Maxine's blog to spy on her, in her world. Now Maxine's "world" was watching them. It was a whole different story now. Now, *their* friends were following along on Maxine's adventures, as she was giving the tea on Ben and Dawn.

It was Ben and Dawn that had become "something to talk about" in a way that they had not imagined. All because of who they'd told about Maxine's blog during their good times. The times *before* Maxine found out about them. It was particularly embarrassing for Ben, because he didn't know who *Maxine had told* about her blog *after* she'd found out about him and Dawn.

While Ben could safely assume she didn't share her blog with her family, Maxine did have lots girlfriends back home that she kept in touch with. He was quite sure her friends were reading the story-and possibly, Michael was reading it as well.

Maybe, she and Michael were lounging in a hotel laughing and snickering behind his and Dawn's backs.

Maxine took great satisfaction in knowing her blog kept Ben and Dawn on edge. Maxine took control and she decided when she had, and they had, had enough.

"Airing their dirty laundry and creating distrust and hurt feelings between them, all the while having them think I didn't know that I was doing it? Are you serious? Priceless!

This has been the most satisfactory get-back that I could have gotten." Maxine thought as she inhaled.

Then she pressed "Publish" on blog entries *"The Tea"* parts #15-17 and exhaled.

Epilogue
"A Queen Rises to the Top"

Maxine the Queen Blogger Plays Chess

Maxine reflected on the months that past. She was proud of the choices that she'd made. She'd gotten things under control and had written her own story, rather than allowed someone else to write it for her.

She didn't get violent. However, she did assert herself and her cleverness to get the best kind of revenge—the kind that would not soon be forgotten.

When all was said and done, Maxine didn't tell Dawn's husband about her affair with Ben. It wasn't that Maxine cared about Dawn or her feelings., Maxine just didn't know what kind of man Dawn was married to.

Maxine was hurt. She was disgusted knowing how weak and stereotypical Ben had proven himself to be. She despised both he and Dawn, but under no circumstance could Maxine condone violence.

Maxine didn't want to put herself, Ben, or Dawn, in danger from someone who might not have the self-control and emotional intelligence that Maxine had.

After a few weeks of not blogging, Maxine and Ben had gone back to their boring routine. They remained co-habitants, living like two strangers though. They didn't have much to say to each other after her last blog-post.

Maxine never really said anything more about his cheating to Ben. She was over it and him.

At that point, Ben didn't have the courage to bring up her blog to her. He'd even stopped dropping "hints" that he knew. He'd gotten that message, that she had known he knew about it for a long time.

While she was highly entertained by keeping Ben and Dawn on their toes, Maxine had other things to think about. She just let them stay uncertain and never really sure if she had chilled or was planning something.

One day after a couple of months had past, Ben told Maxine "You know, it's been over between me and Dawn. It was never really anything in the first place." He added quickly. "You made sure of that. Can't we try to work things out?"

Maxine wasn't sure if he was referencing her visit to Dawn at her job that had made her call it quits with Ben. Or, if they were over because Dawn had read about what he really thought about her.

It didn't matter because Maxine did not want Ben back. Maxine's mission had been accomplished. She had better things to plan now. Ben also continued to ask Maxine to put the money back into their account. Maxine continued to decline to do so.

After the last time he asked about the money, she'd turned to Ben and away from her computer and said, "Consider us even." Ben responded hopefully with "Really? Will that make us even? Are we *really* even now?"

Maxine responded, "Yes, we're even. And, we're also over."

Maxine's eyes had been opened and would never be closed again. She hoped not anyway. Although one could never really be sure in matters of the heart. Maxine thought that it was a little sad that she and Ben ended the way they did.

In some respects, Ben was a decent guy. In other respects, she knew his spinelessness and ability to have his loyalty easily swayed, would not change. His fluidity of spine far over-shadowed his decency when it came to matters-of-the heart. She needed a man who was upright all the time—or at least when it counted to Maxine.

Coming to terms with Ben's true nature, gave her the push she needed to get her life going again somewhere else. It was time to see what "love" would offer her when it's given to and by *someone* else.

Thanks to her blog, she'd been offered a job in another state and was moving for it. *Without Ben.* All she needed to do was sell her house, then she could freely move-on without looking back.

Maxine had really worked hard renovating her house. She'd also spent a lot of money on it but, Ben had brought such disharmony to the house, it was never really the home, she'd envisioned.

Admittedly, Maxine took a little pleasure in telling him she was putting *her* house up for sale, so he should make another living-arrangement ASAP. She didn't even care if it was with Dawn or some other desperate chick.

Maxine was resentful that she was not able to fully enjoy the fruits of her labor, in her own home, for the relatively short time they had lived in it. However, Maxine's renovation efforts paid-off handsomely and quickly. Her house sold in three days.

Knowing that Ben, Dawn, and their friends were reading her blog, she didn't want them to continue to be voyeurs as she moved onto her new life. That meant that she couldn't very well tell her readers where they could find her new blog either.

"Damn Ben and Dawn!" Maxine said aloud as she deleted her blog. Then, she consoled herself with, "Well, if I had to end this blog and start another "Anonymous" one, what better way to do it than by giving Ben and Dawn "the read" of their lives?"

Upon learning it was her last post, many of her readers had left comments saying that they had really enjoyed her stories. They were disappointed to see the blog come to an end.

There was one reader that Maxine corresponded with more frequently than other readers. This reader went by the name of "GG".

GG would encourage Maxine with her enthusiasm for the story and other musings she shared with them. GG would often tell Maxine that she must write a book! Maxine would use this saga as the first step in that undertaking.

Maxine was never much of a Chess player. Yet, with blog at hand, she'd proven that instead of "Maxine, the Broken-Hearted", she was "Maxine, The Queen Blogger".

What about "Anonymous"? Well, that is a whole other story. Maxine began to wonder if she had been taking somethings for granted about "Anonymous". Maybe she'd been looking in the wrong direction…

The End…*For now…*
###

Maxine the Queen Blogger Plays Chess

About the Author

"Naylene" is a citizen of the world. She continues to observe her surroundings quietly and "Anonymously". She recently settled down for a hot-minute, in a much more exciting town to pen some of her adventures. "Maxine The Queen Blogger Plays Chess" is her first novel in a series under the name "Maxine The Queen Blogger".

Naylene can be contacted through Black Swan Publications at: info@blackswanpublications.com Subject line: Naylene

www.ingramcontent.com/pod-product-compliance
Lightning Source LLC
Chambersburg PA
CBHW030313130626
46549CB00002B/836